Something Begins

"I never drove a car before."

"Ever drive a go-kart?"

"Sure."

"If you can drive a go-kart, you can drive this. It's just a bit bigger. Don't worry. I'll teach you. I'm a teacher, remember?"

Something inside me moves, and I find myself stepping out of the car. I watch my shadow stretch tall and merge with Tess's; then it lies briefly beside her, and as I walk around the car, it grows smaller.

Tess climbs into the passenger seat as I get behind the wheel, adjust the seat and mirror like I've watched my parents do all my life. I try to act like I've done this before. For some reason I remember the day I found out about my dad's accident. It just flashes into my head. It's like I relive the whole day in three seconds. All at once I wonder: *Why am I doing this?*

• • •

something
happened

by Greg Logsted

Simon Pulse

New York   London   Toronto   Sydney

This book is a work of fiction. Any references to historical events,
real people, or real locales are used fictitiously. Other names,
characters, places, and incidents are the product of the author's
imagination, and any resemblance to actual events or locales
or persons, living or dead, is entirely coincidental.

SIMON PULSE

An Imprint of Simon & Schuster Children's Publishing Division

1230 Avenue of the Americas, New York, NY 10020

Copyright © 2008 by Greg Logsted

All rights reserved, including the right of reproduction

in whole or in part in any form.

SIMON PULSE and colophon are registered

trademarks of Simon & Schuster, Inc.

Designed by Tom Daly

The text of this book was set in Weiss.

Manufactured in the United States of America

First Simon Pulse edition November 2008

2 4 6 8 10 9 7 5 3 1

Library of Congress Control Number 2008928867

ISBN-13: 978-1-4169-5078-3

ISBN-10: 1-4169-5078-8

For **Jackie** and **Lauren**,
the two halves of my sky

Acknowledgments

A big thank-you to Julia Richardson for picking up the ball, to my editor Liesa Abrams for running with it, and to Pamela Harty, my agent, for being there when I needed her.

I am most grateful for the advice and support of Andrea Schicke Hirsch, Robert Mayette, Krissi Peterson, and Lauren Catherine Simpson.

Jackie for being a patient and inspirational joy.

A special thank-you goes to my wife, Lauren Baratz-Logsted, for being the light that makes all things possible.

Dear Dad,

I can't believe I'm doing this. I can't believe I'm writing to you. It feels strange—really, really strange. It's not like you're ever going to write back or give me a call or anything. It's not like you're going to be driving into our garage again, messing with the garbage cans before trudging up the back stairs, throwing the paper on the table, and giving me a hug like you did for years and years every day after work. No, I don't imagine it's going to be like that. Is it?

I don't even know WHY I'm doing this. I really don't. It's Bragg's idea, of course. Mom keeps saying I've got "issues" and I haven't "properly grieved" and all that other stuff Mom always runs on about. You know how she is and how she gets. So guess what? About four months ago she

1

sent me to this head doctor. Dr. Christopher W. Bragg. He's got an office over by the mall in that ugly brown building. You know the one. You used to call it ugly just about every time we drove by it. She said I needed someone I could "talk" to. Yeah, right. Talk? To him? I can't even get him to tell me what his "W" stands for. He's from Texas, too. I smell a story. What's up with the "W"? Inquiring minds want to know. My money—if I had any—would be on "Wilbur."

Anyhow, Bragg seems to do most of the talking. I thought these guys were supposed to listen and keep quiet and all that. Maybe he doesn't want to be there any more than I do. Could be, right? I know if I was him, I wouldn't want to spend two hours a week locked in a small room trying to "talk" to a thirteen-year-old. He drinks a ton of coffee, too. I think he's struggling to stay awake. His tongue is always brown. I bet they know his first name at the coffee shop. Maybe they even know what the "W" stands for.

Bragg said I should write to you whenever I need to. Like a journal. Tell you what's going on in my life. Tell you my feelings. Tell you I miss you. God, Dad, I do. I miss you so much. I miss you all the time. I miss you so much that it hurts. It's like poison ivy. It's just inside me constantly, this burning and itching feeling of loss. I just can't seem to leave it alone; it's always there just begging me to scratch it. I keep expecting you to walk into the house and announce it was all some kind of a joke. Every time the phone rings, I hope that it's somehow you. Every time I see a car that looks like yours, I check out the driver. Sometimes I'll see a guy your age walking down the street and something about him will look like you, and it's like all the blood in my body just rushes to my head. I stop in my tracks and stare at him, but whatever it was that reminded me of you always melts right away.

I know I have to accept the truth. The stupid, stupid truth. I stood next to Mom at the wake with your open coffin. I stood next to Mom at the cemetery as they lowered your body into the ground. Now I have to stand tall and be brave. Help Mom and the twins. Be the man of the house. Right? That's what you would tell me to do. Isn't it? You'd say, "Billy, wake up. This is the way it is. Deal with it. You have to be a man now."

Dad, I'm sorry I overslept that day. I keep thinking about how I never got to say good-bye. How you got into your car, went off to work, and never came back. I keep thinking that maybe if I had gotten up a little earlier, we would have talked about something. Maybe the Yankees or the weather—you know, anything—and maybe I would have delayed you for just a minute. I figure even just one minute's delay might have been long enough to change everything. One minute is the difference between being in front of the truck or behind it. You were just waiting at a tollbooth. It's not like you were doing anything. Just sitting there waiting. Did you even see the truck coming up behind you? Did you know what was about to happen before it happened? Did you think of us: me and Mom and the twins?

If only I had gotten out of bed. You see, Dad, I didn't really oversleep that day. I was just lazy. I was just lying there listening to my stupid radio. I feel like this was all my fault. I'm sorry.

Well, that's enough for now.

"Good morning! How's my little man? Are you ready for the first day of school?"

I hate when my mom calls me "little man." It was all right when my dad did it, because with him it somehow sounded cool. It made me feel older. It was like, "Hey, it's my little man!" With my mom it makes me feel smaller, younger, less important. Same words, different feelings. Go figure.

"Don't call me 'little man.'"

"Oh, my. Someone got out on the wrong side of the bed this morning."

"Mom, my bed's against the wall. I get out of bed the same side every morning."

"Billy, don't be like this. It's your first day of school. Eighth grade already. I can't believe it—you're growing so fast! Try to think of it as a new beginning."

"It *is* a new beginning. It's the first day of school."

"Just *stop* it, okay?"

"Stop what?"

"You know, the attitude. Just stop. I don't need it right now. Listen, it's going to do you good to get back to school. All you ever do is sit around the house drawing portraits and writing your poems."

"Lyrics, Mom. I told you, they're lyrics, not poems."

"Doesn't matter. The point is, you have to get out of the house. Did you eat?"

"Yeah, toast and jam."

"You've got to start eating more for breakfast. You hear me?"

"Yeah."

"What are you drawing?"

She comes over to the kitchen table, stands by my side, and leans over my sketch pad.

"Hey, it's me! Wow, Billy, that's really, really good. I'm not just saying that because you're my kid. My eyes, my hair, my mouth—it's perfect. Save this one for me, okay? Look, you even have me wearing my new Bluetooth!"

My mom sells real estate. She's been the top seller at her office for three straight years now. It seems like her cell phone is on all day long. She's always taking or making calls. I hate that Bluetooth; she wears it all day long too. I never know when she's on or off the phone. She'll be doing something with me, and then she'll just start talking to someone. It always takes me a moment to realize she's not talking to me.

"Did you dress and feed the twins?"

"Yes, Mother."

"I told you, don't give me that attitude."

"Okay."

"What are they doing now?"

"Watching *The Wiggles*."

She looks toward the living room. A muffled song is coming from that direction. She pulls out the chair next to me, sits down, and lowers her voice.

"Did you read that book I gave you last night?"

This summer we went to four different churches. I'm not sure why. One day Mom just decided it was time for us to start going to church again, but she didn't want to go to the one we used to go to with Dad. I kind of liked the church we went to with Dad. Mom thought it would be too painful.

She must have picked up the book she gave me yesterday at one of those churches. She told me to read it late at night when everyone was asleep. It's called *Almost Twelve*. When I told her I was thirteen, she told me that it didn't matter. Basically, it's a book about sex. The thing is, it was like reading a book about how to make a bomb, but every page was also telling you how dangerous bombs are and never to make one. When I finished it, I think I had more questions than answers.

I lower my voice to match hers. "Yeah, I read it."

"Do you have any questions?"

I'm kind of embarrassed by this sudden "talk." Maybe if I'd had some more time to prepare myself, I'd be able to just dive in. But this is, like, all at once. Besides, my bus should be coming soon and I don't want to miss it.

"Well, not really . . . uh, maybe some. I guess."

"Really? You have some questions?" She clears her throat.

"Well . . . um . . . not a lot."

"You know . . . if you have any questions . . . you could ask me."

In a sudden, singsong voice my mother chimes, like I've heard her chime hundreds of times before, "Mary O'Hara-Romero, Prestige Real Estate. May I help you?"

Again it throws me. For a second I think she's trying to be funny.

"Yes, Nancy. It's a four-bedroom colonial. Beautiful house, and the owners are very motivated to sell. I think this could be just what we've been looking for."

I throw up my arms, roll my eyes, and stand up. I can't help it.

My mom holds up her finger for me to wait a second.

"Nancy, I'm going to have to put you on hold for just a moment. Okay?" She looks at me. "Billy, don't be like this. We'll talk, I promise. Okay, hon? Besides, shouldn't you have been at the bus stop by now?"

I look at the clock. She's right. I run over to the closet, grab my backpack, and throw in my sketch pad and notebook. Then I hear the bus coming up the hill. My mom hears it too.

"You better not miss that bus! I've got a meeting this morning, and I don't have time to drive you to school, on top of taking the twins to preschool."

I yell good-bye to my mom and fly out the side door. The screen door slams behind me. I see the bus coming up the street, and I know if I run as fast as I can, I'll just make it.

I'm struggling to catch my breath and my legs feel like rubber bands when I finally walk down the aisle. The bus is packed. I don't recognize anyone from last year. I look for Ziggy. We've been sitting together for years. He isn't there either. For a moment I panic and think I'm on the wrong bus, but no, it's the right number. They must have just changed the route.

I take the only open seat. It's next to this beautiful girl that I've never seen before. Maybe she moved into town over the summer. She looks at me briefly when I sit down, but then turns back to the window.

I want to say something to her. Anything. We sit together in what seems like a thick fog of silence for miles. I keep running stupid ideas through my head. Maybe I should say this; maybe I should say that. Finally I realize I should just keep it simple. Just say hi and tell her my name.

That's all I have to do, just say hi. Why can't I get myself to do even that? What am I waiting for? Why am I such a wimp? I hate being like this.

Time is running out. We're getting closer to school. We'll be there in a few minutes. If I don't say something now, it's going to be too late.

Two summers ago I was at this cliff at Great Pond with some friends. It must have been at *least* fifteen feet high. Everyone was jumping in and seemed to be having a blast. When it was my time to jump, I just stood there looking down. I couldn't get myself to do it. I wanted to, but I kept thinking about all the things that might go wrong. Maybe I'd hit a rock. Maybe I'd land wrong and break something, or knock myself out and drown. Maybe this; maybe that.

My friends started chanting, "Jump, jump, jump."

I wanted to jump. I wanted to launch myself off the rocks. To feel the wind rushing by me. To feel for the briefest moment that I was flying, that I was free. To feel that I had conquered my fears and was just as brave as my friends. But most of all I wanted that feeling of having totally committed myself to something. To jump and to know that there was no turning back. To know that whatever happened when I hit the water, at least I'd had the courage to jump.

I couldn't jump that day. I couldn't look my friends in the eye. I crawled back down the rocks; it was a slow and humiliating process. I got on my bike and rode home.

I decide that today, on this bus, I am finally going to jump.

I turn to her. I imagine myself pushing off the rocks, sailing through the air, rushing toward the water, and I say in a voice that is way too loud, "Hi, me name's Billy Romero!"

She actually jumps in her seat and turns to me with a wide-eyed, startled expression. I'm such an idiot. Why did I shout? What's wrong with me? "Me name's"? Did I really say "me name's"? I can't even say a simple hello.

She lowers her voice and mumbles something before looking out the window again.

The bus is pulling into the school's parking lot. I reach out and gently touch her shoulder. "What? I'm sorry. What did you say? I couldn't hear you."

She rolls her eyes. "I said, my name's Amy Wilson and you have strawberry jam on your chin."

She gathers her stuff.

I start to smile. It doesn't matter. It doesn't matter that I shouted. It doesn't matter that I have strawberry jam on my face or that I said "me" instead of "my." All that matters is that I found the courage to jump.

Dear Dad,

Well, I finished my first week of school. I thought it would be easy to slip back into it. I was wrong—it was really, really tough. I had no idea it would be like that. I thought that after the long summer maybe having a "structured routine" would be good for me. That's what Bragg kept saying. He said "structured routine" so many times that it started to sound like my personal password to happiness. But so far my "structured routine" has not led to happiness. I felt like I spent the whole week in slow motion, while everyone else rushed by me in their own separate time zones. I just seemed to be moving through this thick paste all day long.

Last year was tough too, but at least my friends and teachers were understanding and supportive. Now I can tell that everyone thinks of your death as something that happened in that distant past known as "last year." We weren't in seventh grade a year ago; we were in seventh grade three months ago. We weren't in seventh grade last year; we were in seventh grade this year. My friend Ziggy was telling someone that my father died "last year." I wanted to shout that it was just five months ago, not a year ago!

My teachers are telling me I've got to keep focused in class. My friends don't understand why I don't feel like playing their stupid games. All around me I see people laughing, joking, and walking around with these huge, goofy smiles plastered on their faces. I've begun to wonder how they do it, and more important, will I ever be able to be like that again? It's like I fell into this deep, dark hole and everyone came to help but they didn't stay very long. I guess I didn't climb out quickly enough; they got bored and left me to climb alone in the dark.

Anyway, it's not all bad. For one thing, I met this girl on the bus. Her name's Amy Wilson. I like her. She's not my girlfriend or anything like that; she's just a friend. She saves me a seat on the bus every morning and we talk, or I should say we try to talk. Oh, she's also really cute.

My teachers are all nice too. You know, normally I'll

have one or two that I'm not crazy about, but this year I
like them all. My English teacher is so cool! She seems really
young, too. When I first saw her walking into the classroom,
I thought she was another kid. She isn't very tall. This is
her first year teaching. Her name is Miss Tess Gate. She
said we could call her Tess around the classroom because
"Miss Gate" sounds too much like "mistake," and she
doesn't want any mistakes in her classroom if she can avoid
them. She is by far the best-looking teacher I've ever had.
It's really hard to believe she's a teacher. Long, brown hair,
blue eyes, and she even looks a bit like Angelina Jolie.

The first thing she did that's really cool happened
when I went to her class and she called out attendance.
When she was finished, she asked if anyone's name
hadn't been called. I raised my hand, and she came to
my desk, squatted down next to me, and asked to see my
schedule. She quickly looked at it, then wrote me a short
note on the back of a hall pass. It said, "Billy, you're
supposed to be in my sixth-period class. This is fifth period.
You should be in Mr. Chilton's history class, room 105. See
you soon. Good luck."

Then she stood up, gave me a quick wink, and said
loud enough for the class to hear, "Billy, there seems to be

a problem with your schedule. Why don't you go to guidance and have them check it out."

Most teachers don't seem to care if they embarrass you in front of everybody. Some even seem to enjoy it, but she's different. I was having a tough day and she really made a difference.

Well, I'm hoping the weekend will help get me on track for next week. We'll see.

My locker is way back by the shop classes, and it takes me forever to get there. On my way out to the bus I remember that I have a history quiz tomorrow and my book is in my locker. I think I'll have plenty of time to make it there and back. I even run.

I'm wrong. When I come outside, the first bus in line is starting to move. I frantically run to the row of buses and take a gamble, thinking my bus will be on the left-hand side like it normally is. I'm wrong again: Today it must have been on the right.

It doesn't really sink in that I've missed the bus until I watch the last one pull out and head down the street. There's a garbage can next to me, and I really feel like just running and kicking it over. Just want to give it a big, angry kick, followed by an ear-piercing frustrated scream. Maybe jump on top of it a few times too until it's all flat and dented. But I realize that would be pointless. Although I can't resist giving it a small kick when I go by. It makes a loud, hollow *thud* sound.

I walk back toward the front door. I don't even have a cell phone. This is what I've been talking about. I keep telling my mother that I *need* a cell phone. If I had a cell phone right now, all I'd have to do is reach into my backpack, take it out, and give my mom a call and that would be that.

Luckily I have a pocket full of change, and there's a pay phone just inside the main door.

Some girl I don't recognize is using the phone, so I stand behind her and wait. She's talking so fast I start to feel like a wave of paste is about to wash over me.

"So it was like why am I even here? You know what I mean? Paul is talking to Jenny. Tim is talking to Sue, and I'm just sitting there with nobody talking to me. You know what I mean? I felt like standing on the table and shouting, 'Hello? Does anybody even know I'm alive?' What's wrong with people? You know what I mean? After that you'll never guess what Jenny actually has the nerve to say . . ."

The girl turns and looks at me standing there and says into the phone, "Hold on a sec, okay?" She looks at me harder. "Can I help you?"

"Um, I just need to use the phone."

"I'm using it now."

"Um, I can see you're using it, but I only need it for a second. I missed the bus, and I need to call my mother."

"I'll be off in a few minutes. I'm right in the middle of something."

"It's just for a second to call my mother."

The girl gives me an angry stare. "Listen, ever hear of first-come, first-served? Can't you see I got the phone first? You can have it when I'm finished."

She turns her back to me and continues with her conversation. "I don't know. Some loser. He wants me to hang up. Yeah, you got that right . . . is he cute?" She gives me a glance. "Not really."

I move away from the phone and sit on the floor just inside the door, where I can keep an eye on the phone. I have a feeling it's going to be a long wait. Even though I've never seen this girl before, her "Not really" comment really hurts. Who would have thought that two words from a stranger could take so much life out of a person?

Anyway, as long as I'm waiting, I figure I'll draw her. Drawing always helps me relax. I think I'll make her about fifty pounds overweight and with a mouth the size of Texas.

I grab my pad and start sketching. First an outline of her body, with the extra pounds of course. Her hair, her beady eyes, her huge mouth talking into the phone (that part's funny), can't forget the pimple on her chin, may as well make it larger, and now I'll fill in the details so you can tell who she is. Maybe I'll tack it onto the main bulletin board when I'm finished.

"Hey, that's really good."

Miss Gate is standing by my side, looking at the drawing. I didn't even hear her walk up to me. She must have changed. She's not wearing the dress she had on in class today. Now she's wearing jeans, a Red Hot Chili Peppers T-shirt, and boots. She also has her hair down; she normally wears it up. I hardly recognize her.

"Oh, hi, Miss Gate."

"Tess."

"Oh yeah, um . . . hi . . . Tess."

She raises her chin and points it at the girl on the phone. "You mad at her or something?"

"Who?"

"Judy Hall."

"Who's Judy Hall?"

"That's the girl you're drawing the picture of. She's in my third-period class. You're really ripping her apart in your drawing."

I close my sketch pad and mumble, "Well, yeah, I guess."

"What did she do?"

I can't keep the anger out of my voice. "Do? It's more like what she's not doing. She's been on the phone forever, and she's not letting me use it. She just talks and talks and talks. I'm sick of all this. Doesn't anybody think of anyone but themselves? I just don't get it. I have to call my mother, I missed the bus, and why does this school have only one pay phone? Tell me that makes sense."

Tess puts her hand on my shoulder. "I know how you feel. I can't get her to stop talking in class, either."

She reaches into her bag and then hands me a cell phone. "Here, why don't you just use this?"

I call my mom.

"Mary O'Hara-Romero, Prestige Real Estate. May I help you?"

"Hi, it's me."

"Billy, is something wrong?"

"I missed my bus. Can you pick me up?"

"Oh, that's just great. How do you miss a bus?"

"I forgot a book in my locker. I thought I could make it . . ."

My mother lets out a long sigh. "I can't. I've got a showing in about ten minutes. I'm waiting for the client now."

"Well, how long before you can get here?"

"I don't know. An hour at the earliest, and that's pushing it."

"More than an hour! What am I supposed to do for an hour? Mom, can't you just—"

Tess taps my shoulder and motions for me to give her the phone.

"Mom, my English teacher wants to talk to you. Her name's Miss Gate."

I hand her the phone. She flicks her hair back and places it to her ear. "Hello, Mrs. Romero. . . . I'm sorry, Mrs. *O'Hara*-Romero. . . . Okay, Mary. This is Tess Gate, Billy's English teacher. . . . Fine, how are you? . . . Oh, I'm sorry to hear that. . . . Yes, I know what that's like. . . . I've been there, done that. . . . Yes, yes, tell me about it."

She laughs about something my mother says.

"Listen, Mary, if you want, I can drive Billy home, it's on my way. . . . No, really, it's not a problem. . . . Okay, then. . . . Sure. . . . Okay. . . . It was great talking to you, Mary. Have a nice day. Bye."

She turns to me and smiles. "Problem solved. Let's go for a ride."

"Wow! Is this your car?"

We're standing next to a brand-new red Mustang convertible. It's my dream car. If I were a car, I would want to be this one.

She smiles. "Sure is. Hop in."

I open the door, throw my stuff in the back, and jump into the front seat. It feels great; it even smells great, a combo of new-car smell and perfume.

Tess slips behind the wheel and puts the key in the ignition, and the engine roars to life.

"Want me to put the top down?"

"Yeah, that would be cool."

I can't remember the last time I drove in a convertible. I love the way the fresh air rushes in and the sky slowly opens up above us.

"How's that seat for you? You're fairly tall. You might want to push it back a bit. It's over here." She reaches across me and shows me how to move my seat back.

"Do you like Beck?" she asks while slipping in a CD.

"I love Beck. He's my favorite."

"I thought you might."

We inch out of the parking space and drift through the parking lot. Passing the school and slowly cruising up the driveway. The car's engine seems to be begging to go faster. It's rumbling, straining, growling in frustration at the sluggish pace. We turn left onto the main road, and when we're around the corner and out of sight of the school, she steps on the gas while turning up the music. Soon Beck is thumping and the wind is in our hair. Trees and mailboxes zip past us. The car hugs the corners and explodes down the straightaways. I look over at Tess. The wind is whipping the hair around her face, her eyes are focused, her hands are firmly on the wheel, and I can see the muscles flexing in her arms. She looks calm, confident, and totally in control of this fast and powerful car. The music is loud and wonderful. I smile.

We drive past someone on a bike. Hey, it's my friend Ziggy. We briefly make eye contact. We're moving too fast for me to wave.

There's a picture of my dad that I love. It's hanging on the wall in the den. He's around seventeen. His hair is long, he's smiling and looking straight into the camera. He's wearing a tan turtleneck sweater, faded jeans, and sneakers.

His arms are crossed; he looks young, strong, and very happy. He's leaning against his "favorite car of all time," a 1968 Mustang fastback.

He told me the story of when he first bought the car. He'd heard about it from a friend of a friend. Then talked his own dad into driving him sixty miles to check it out. He had $3,000 in his pocket. Thirty crisp, new hundred-dollar bills. He fell in love with the car the moment he saw it in the driveway. The engine could have sounded like a dryer full of boots, spare change, and broken bottles; smoke could have spilled out from underneath and covered them in a thick black cloud; and he still would have bought it.

They test-drove it, and the engine sounded as good as the car looked. My dad was ready to buy it right then, just hand over his $3,000 and drive home. His dad took over and saved him $600.

Dad said the drive home was a feeling he'd never forget. A mixture of pride and excitement. He said he didn't believe he'd ever again enjoy driving a car as much as he did that day. When he arrived home, he drove straight to the beach to show it off. That's when he met my mother. She claims to have noticed my father before his car, but my dad never believed it. Who would?

Tess looks over at me and shouts over the music, "What are you thinking about? You look miles away."

I shout back, "I was just thinking that I love this car!"

Tess slams on the brakes, the car fishtails to the left, she takes a hard turn, and we sail up a short driveway, past an abandoned factory, and into a huge, empty parking lot.

When we get to the middle of the lot, she stops, gets out, and leaves her door open, the engine running.

I'm confused. What's going on? Why is she getting out of the car?

She walks around the car and opens my door. Her shadow stretches across the lot like a dark giant lying on the pavement.

"Why don't you take her for a spin?"

"What?"

"Take the car for a ride."

"But I don't have a license."

She holds out her arms and spins around; the dark pavement giant spins along with her. "There's nothing here. You don't need a license for a closed parking lot."

"But I'm only thirteen."

"You're old enough. Besides, it's an automatic; they practically drive themselves. Come on, we're in the middle of an empty parking lot. It's not like it's a road or highway or anything."

"I never drove a car before."

"Ever drive a go-kart?"

"Sure."

"If you can drive a go-kart, you can drive this. It's just

a bit bigger. Don't worry. I'll teach you. I'm a teacher, remember?"

Something inside me moves, and I find myself stepping out of the car. I watch my shadow stretch tall and merge with Tess's; then it lies briefly beside her, and as I walk around the car, it grows smaller.

Tess climbs into the passenger seat as I get behind the wheel, adjust the seat and mirror like I've watched my parents do all my life. I try to act like I've done this before. For some reason I remember the day I found out about my dad's accident. It just flashes into my head. It's like I relive the whole day in three seconds. All at once I wonder: *Why am I doing this?*

Tess puts her hand on my shoulder. "Don't be nervous. You can do this. It'll be fun."

I take a deep breath to steady my nerves. I turn to Tess. She has a huge smile, and I can see excitement in her eyes. "I'm not nervous."

Her smile grows even larger. "Okay! Let's get started. Put on your seat belt."

I slip the belt across my chest and click it into place. My hands are shaking, but I don't think she notices.

"Now, this is what I want you to do. First let out the e brake. Then I want you to very gently touch the gas, drive ten feet, then step on the brake; drive ten feet, then step on the brake. Keep doing that all the way across the lot. That will help you get a feel for the car. Got it?"

I do that for about fifteen minutes. At first the car is very jumpy, but then I seem to get it all at once. When I get to the point where I'm smoothly starting and stopping, Tess says, "Okay, now go ahead and drive slowly around the parking lot, nice big circles and figure eights."

I'm doing it! I'm driving a car—I can't believe it! Big circles around the parking lot, figure eights, back and forth. I feel like I'm floating. The engine feels alive, like a caged beast. I love the feeling of being in control.

I wonder what will happen if I step on the gas hard for just a second. The car jumps forward like a cat pouncing on a mouse. It scares and excites me at the same time.

Tess pats my shoulder. "Relax. It's important to relax . . . and don't forget to enjoy yourself."

I do begin to relax. I push the bad thoughts away. I let myself enjoy this moment, my moment. I love the feel of the wheel in my hands, the feeling of power when I press the gas pedal down. I never thought I would love driving a car this much. I thought it would be great, but I didn't realize it would be this great.

Now I understand why my dad would go on and on about his first car and that first drive. I wonder if I'll talk about this day twenty years from now. It's funny how things turn out. Growing up, I just always thought it would be my dad who would teach me how to drive. I wonder if he would

ne here. I can't think of any closer parking lots
e. I wonder how he would have taught me. I
. well, I wonder about so many things lately.
What good does it do me? It's just not fair, even on this day;
it's just not fair.

"Billy . . .

"Billy . . .

Tess is looking at me. "Are you okay?"

"Yeah, I'm fine. Just got a little something in my eye."

I stop the car and put it in park.

"You can drive longer if you want."

"No. I feel good with what I did. For my first time . . .
well, I feel good."

"Sure, you did really good. Did you have fun?"

"Yeah, thanks." I get out of the car and walk around it.
I watch my shadow grow larger again. I open and hold the
door for Tess.

"Why, thank you, sir."

"You're welcome, madam."

We fly out of the parking lot and cruise around the lake.
The sun does this wild dance on the water. Thousands of
sparkling little diamonds. The music seems to play right
along with the dancing diamonds. I look over at Tess, and I
feel like I'm in a music video. We shoot up Mountain Road;
deer run through the woods, jumping over logs and bushes.
When we get to the top of the road, I can see the whole town

spread out below us. It doesn't look real, more like those little model towns they build for low-budget monster movies. I can imagine Godzilla stomping down Main Street, heading toward my school. Now, that would be a great movie.

When we get to the long, straight section of River Road, Tess punches the gas and we roar down the street. Two fishermen watch us; they both smile. I wonder if they're smiling at Tess or the car. I'm willing to bet it's both, but more Tess than the car.

We round the familiar corner at the end of my street. Tess slows the car down to a crawl. A few moments later she pulls up in front of my house and turns the engine off. Somehow my house looks a bit different.

Tess turns and looks at me. I suddenly feel uncomfortable. She reaches out and places her hand on my shoulder and looks me in the eye. "Listen, before you go, I want to tell you something."

"Okay." I swallow hard. Why does she have her hand on my shoulder?

"I have to tell you that I read your records. Well, I read all my students' records, but . . . I wanted to say that they mention what happened. You know . . . um, the accident. I'm really sorry that you lost your father last spring. I know how very, very painful this is. I'm not just saying this. You see, when I was your age, I lost my father too. He had a heart attack at the breakfast table.

"My friends were there for me in the beginning, offering help and a shoulder to cry on, but they quickly moved on with their lives. I spent a lot of time alone and in pain. I felt angry and cheated, but mainly I felt like there was this huge, empty void where there used to be a playful, fun-loving girl. I'm just telling you this because if you want someone to talk to, anytime—and I mean anytime—I'm here for you. Okay?"

She gives me a quick hug.

I'm starting to feel like I'm about to cry. I feel like a bag of water that's just been sliced down the side. I've got to get out of this car now. I've got to run or I'm just going to start crying, and if I start, I know I'll never stop. I can't let her see me like that. My bottom lip begins to shake. I mutter, "Thank you," before bolting out of the car and down to my house.

Dear Dad,

What a day. It's funny how days, weeks, even months, can pass without much happening, and then a day will come along so jam-packed with stuff that it feels like its own separate year. The big news is I drove a car—a brand-new Mustang! You would have loved this car. It's so nice. I understand now why you loved Mustangs so much. What a beautiful car. When I get my license, I want one. You see, what happened was, I missed the bus, my English teacher gave me a ride home, and on the way she decided to give me a driving lesson in the old Wireside parking lot. I think I did great. You would have been proud. She said we could do it again sometime. That would be cool.

I've been hanging with Ziggy a bit more. We hadn't

been doing all that much together the last couple of months. I'm not sure why. I think it's my fault. Whenever he would call, I'd make up some excuse. Also, Ziggy's got his girlfriends, so it's not like he's sitting around waiting for me to call. I still can't believe how the girls just fall all over him. Remember that time we all went out to that restaurant, and the girl at the next table just gave Ziggy her phone number without him even asking for it? You jokingly said that he was a valuable friend to have around. I think I finally get what you meant.

I wish I were more like Ziggy. Whenever I try to talk to a girl, something happens to my brain. I think they have secret powers and they're able to make a guy act stupid simply by looking at him. It's like my brain short-circuits or something; it slows down like a virus-infected computer. I wonder why I can't just act normal.

I do all right talking to that girl Amy from my bus. When I talk to her, my brain isn't infested with thought-numbing viruses; it's more like a maze of pop-up ads. I can deal with pop-up ads so long as there aren't too many of them. Besides, it doesn't seem to bother her when I say really stupid things; she thinks it's funny. In fact

What's that? I thought I heard something. Is someone calling me? I'm working on my Dad Journal. I cross my room and turn down the Foo Fighters, stand still. No, I don't hear anything. It must have been part of the music. Something that just sounded like my name.

"Billy!"

Nope, it's my mom. Why does she do that? Just stand at the bottom of the stairs and yell. It's not like we live in a mansion. She could just walk fifteen feet up and knock on my door, or pound, depending upon the volume of what I'm listening to.

I go to the landing and lean over the railing.

"What?"

"I've been yelling and yelling."

"If I had a cell phone, you could just call me."

"You're not getting a cell phone."

I start to walk back to my room.

"Billy!"

I lean back over the railing. "What."

"I'm calling you."

"Yes, the old-fashioned way."

"Enough already. Come downstairs. There's somebody who wants to see you."

"Who?"

"Just get down here. You're being rude."

"I'm being rude? You're the one shouting like it's New Year's Eve."

"Billy!"

"Okay, okay. I'm coming." I run down the stairs.

My mother is looking in the hall mirror, patting her hair. "She's in the living room."

"She?"

I walk into the room and see Miss Gate sitting on the beige sofa with her legs crossed and a cup of tea in her lap. It's so strange to see her here. Wow, she's even changed since this afternoon. Back to wearing a dress, with her hair up. Her basic teacher's costume; she's even wearing her glasses.

She looks up and smiles. "Hello, Billy."

"Miss Gate, what are you doing here?"

My mom walks up behind me. "Billy, is that any way to talk to your teacher? You should be thanking Miss Gate. You forgot your backpack and sketch pad in her car this afternoon, and she was kind enough to bring them over. You know, she didn't have to do that."

Tess waves her hand at my mother. "Mary, it was nothing. I was driving right by anyhow—I already told you that."

"Still, Billy, I think you owe Miss Gate a thank-you."

"Thank you, Miss Gate."

She raises an eyebrow above her glasses. "Like I said, no problem."

My mom sits next to Tess, leaving me just standing in the middle of the room, wondering if I should stay or go. She clears her throat. "Listen, Miss Gate was telling me something exciting. She said she came across some of your poems in your sketch pad."

Tess puts down her cup of tea. "I hope you don't mind, Billy. I just saw your sketch pad and wanted to take another look at that picture of Judy Hall. I came across the poems by mistake."

I just stand there. This isn't good. I don't want anyone reading my lyrics. I write them for myself. Oh, who am I fooling? They're poems, not lyrics. Which ones do I have in there, anyway? This is so embarrassing. I do a quick review of what's in there. Oh, God. I don't want anyone reading that one, or that one either. There are lots of poems I don't want anyone reading. Why did she do that? What drawings are in there? Oh no! No, no, no, I made up one of Tess the other night! I don't know why, just fantasizing, I guess. I sketched her lying naked on my bed with only a small towel covering part of her body. I meant to take that one out. Mom called me for dinner. I forgot about it. How could I do that? I'm so stupid. Did she see that one? Why did I do that? I'm so stupid, stupid, stupid. What if that's why she's really here? Maybe she's going to show it to my mother. Tell her what a pervert her son is. The blood is rushing to my head. I can actually feel my face getting red. I'm dizzy. Is it hot in here? What if I pass out? It could happen, right? I could pass out. Just like that, standing one second, rushing toward the floor the next. Crash right across the coffee table, knock Tess's tea all over the carpet. Maybe even split my head open. Stop thinking about it. Stop it. Stop it right now.

My mother jumps in. "She says they're really, really good. She thinks they could be published. Isn't that right, Tess?"

"Oh, yes, definitely. I even know some contests you should consider entering too. They need to be polished a bit, but you really have some good stuff here."

I'm still standing. Am I swaying a bit, like a tree in a storm? I really should say something, anything. She must have seen the picture. Even if she didn't, some of those poems are really embarrassing. Say something. Just say something, but try to sound calm.

"Um, those poems aren't really ready to be read. They're just, you know, well, kinda like shadows . . . shadows without bodies."

Tess reaches for her tea. Takes a sip and looks at me over her glasses. Her eyes somehow seem to be a brighter blue tonight. They look different, separate from her body, almost like they have their own language. I feel like they're pulling me, demanding something from me that I don't understand. I tell myself to look away, but for some reason I don't feel like I can.

She smiles, a little smile, more like just the corners of her mouth. "'Shadows without bodies'?"

She turns to my mom. "'Shadows without bodies.' See what I mean, Mary? Your son has a real talent with words."

"Well, he is always working on something inside that sketch pad of his. You really think he has talent?"

"Oh, yes. As a matter of fact, I wanted to ask you something. I belong to this poetry workshop. It has a nice mix of teens and adults. We meet Friday nights at Jumping Java's. If Billy wants to improve his poetry, this might be a good place to start. It's a friendly group, and I think he'd fit right in and get a lot out of it."

My mom looks at me. I know that look—she's thinking.

Why am I still standing? I should sit down. I sit on the floor in front of the coffee table. Why did I do that? Sit on the floor like that? Children sit on the floor. I should have sat on a chair, like an adult. Is it too late to move? Oh, just stay here; don't go bouncing around like a little puppy. That would look even worse.

My mom turns to Tess. "Well, I guess we'd have to talk about the details, but it's really up to Billy. Hon, is this something you think—Mary O'Hara-Romero, Prestige Real Estate. May I help you?"

I don't believe it. Why does she do that? Can't she turn that stupid phone off? I look at Tess. She seems confused.

"Oh, yes, Julie. Of course I remember you. How are

you? . . . I'm doing well myself. . . . I know I have something in your price range. As a matter of fact, something just came on the market this morning that I think would be perfect for you."

My mom holds up her finger to us and mouths, "Just a second." Then she walks out of the room.

Tess looks at me and whispers, "Wow, right in the middle of our conversation. At first I thought she was losing her mind."

I burst out laughing but quickly cover my mouth and try to control myself. I whisper back, "I know what you mean. It drives everyone crazy. One time at the bank she was cashing a check, and the teller didn't know she was on the phone, and my mom says, 'It's four hundred and fifty thousand,' and the teller just looks at her and says, 'No, it's not; it's for a hundred and eighty bucks.'"

Tess's laugh is louder than mine, almost like a bark. Both of her hands shoot up to her mouth. She seems to be laughing through her nose. It almost sounds painful.

I go in for the kill. "Another time we were at the Dunkin' Donuts drive-through and my mom was talking to some contractor, and when she drove up to the window, she said, 'I ordered two toilets and a shower door.' The guy just looked at her and said, 'Ma'am, you ordered two glazed donuts and a cup of coffee.'"

This time Tess's laugh is explosive, like when you

accidentally step on a dog's tail. She waves her hands at me to stop. She tries to hold the laughter inside, her whole body is shaking, her eyes are watering. She's making this snorting, honking sound.

In between snorts she hisses, "Billy, please stop. You're going to get me in trouble."

I'm tempted to tell her about that time at the post office.

She waves her hand at me. "No more, I mean it."

"Okay, okay."

We control our laughter and replace it with an awkward silence that starts to stretch on far too long. I wonder if she found that picture I drew of her. She's not acting like she saw it. I think if she did, she might say something. Then again, maybe she missed it, or if she did see it, she might have thought it wasn't her. I bet that's it. After all, the face wasn't that clear. I always seem to get everybody's eyes all wrong too.

In the other room we can hear my mother making her pitch. "Oh yes, it actually has three bathrooms. Big bathrooms. The master bathroom is a dream. You could practically live in it . . . ."

I look at my hands; they're in my lap. I'm sitting with my legs crossed, feeling foolish again for sitting on the floor.

"Miss Gate—"

She waves her finger at me. "It's Tess."

"Okay . . . Tess . . ." Using her first name feels really

strange to me, like wearing my best suit to weed the garden. "I don't know about this poetry-coffee-shop thing. I don't even drink coffee."

"Oh, you don't have to drink coffee. Don't worry about that."

"Well, yeah, I know, but it's not really the coffee part I'm worried about, it's the whole thing. I'm not that sure I want to read my poetry in front of people. I think I'd be too nervous."

"There's nothing to worry about. What's the worst thing that could happen?"

"Worst thing?"

"Yes, let's start from there. What's the worst thing that could possibly happen?"

I think about it for a moment. "Well, I guess I could pass out, fall through a plate glass window, and a big piece of glass could come crashing down and cut my head off. I guess that would be the worst thing that could possibly happen."

Tess looks like she's going to laugh again but controls herself. "That's not going to happen."

"Well, it could."

"Only in some sick graphic novel. Come on, really, what's the worst thing that could *realistically* happen?"

"Well, I guess people could laugh at me."

"Guess what? That's not going to happen either. You know how I know that?"

"How?"

"A couple of reasons. You have some great poems, and people love to hear a great poem. Also, I know everyone in the group, and they're not the kind of people to laugh at somebody." Tess adjusts her glasses. "Listen, three weeks ago this new guy stood up, hands shaking like a leaf, and read a truly awful poem about his long-lost dog. Nobody laughed at him. Like I said, it's just not that type of group. It's very, very supportive."

"But I'm not even sure I want to read one of my poems."

"Well, nobody's going to force you to. This is all I'm saying: You have a great talent; you should do something with it. If you don't use it, you'll lose it. I was nervous the first time I read one of my poems, but I was so glad I did. It helped a great deal, and it was also, believe it or not, a lot of fun."

"Fun?"

"Yes, there's something exciting about sharing something you created and then having other people show their approval."

"Well, I don't know . . ."

Tess suddenly leans forward, startling me into pulling back, but she just keeps coming, at last gently brushing my hair out of my eyes with her fingers. It's the kind of thing only my mother has done before. "Don't worry. I'll help you. We'll make sure you blow everyone away. It'll be fun, you'll see. Maybe we'll even find some spare time for another driving lesson."

My mother walks back into the room, talking as she walks; it takes me a second to realize she's talking to us again. "So. I'm sorry about that. I really had to take that call; I've been waiting for her to call me back for hours. It looks like it might be worth the wait, too. She wants to both buy and sell."

Tess leans back into the sofa, picking up her teacup in the process, then smiles. "That is good news. I've got some more good news. I think Billy wants to move forward with his writing."

"I want you to tell me one more time about the phone call."

Again with the phone call? What's up with Bragg? I'm beginning to think that psychiatrists drive people crazy. It's one of those "Which came first?" things, the chicken or the egg.

I'm sitting in this weird chair that I always sit in when I come here. Well, I don't really have a choice. Bragg sits in his leather chair, and I sit in the pillow-type chair across from him. It looks normal enough, but the longer you sit in it, the lower you seem to sink. Our meeting must be getting close to the end because my chin is where my chest used to be. I feel like one of those California lowriders. I need my shades, man.

"Dr. Bragg, I've told you twice about the stupid phone call. Can't we give it a rest already?"

"Indulge me one last time. I want to make sure we get all the details straight. What room were you in when the phone rang?"

"The kitchen."

"Were you alone?"

"Yeah, I told you. Everyone was out."

"How many times did it ring?"

"Twice, I think."

"Then what did you do?"

"Do? I picked up the phone and said hello."

"And someone said hello right back to you?"

"No. I said hello and no one said anything, but I could tell someone was there."

"How did you know that?"

"Because I could hear all these background noises— plates and glasses clinking, people talking, music playing— and also because I could hear someone breathing."

"Someone breathing? You didn't mention that before."

I push myself up in the seat; if I slide down much more, I'll be sitting on the floor. "I forgot or didn't think it was important or something."

"Billy, I want you to tell me everything about the phone call. Tell me what was said and how you felt. Last time, I promise."

"Okay, I'm listening to the background noises and I'm thinking that maybe it's my mom calling from a restaurant

44

or bar or something, I don't know. So I say, 'Hello? Hello? Is anybody there?' I say that three or four times, and then I'm about to hang up, but I don't. I don't know why. I just hang on for a while and listen to the breathing and the background noises. I feel . . . puzzled, I guess. Then I say, 'All right, nice talking to ya, good-bye.' But just when I'm about to hang up, a man asks, 'Are you Billy Romero?'

"I don't know why, but it kinda scared me at first. So I didn't say anything. Just listened. I heard a plate break in the background and someone laugh and a couple other muffled sounds. It felt like I waited a really long time, but it was probably only about fifteen seconds, maybe less. Finally I said, 'Yeah, who is this?' He cleared his throat. 'Uh, it's Ryan Murphy.'"

Bragg scratches the top of his head with his pen. "Did you recognize the name?"

"No, not really. I didn't recognize it, but it's like I could feel it."

"Feel it?"

"Yeah, hearing the name was like being instantly covered with a wet, heavy blanket. I could feel the weight of it. I could feel the dread of it. I could feel the darkness that surrounded it. I didn't want anything to do with that name."

"What did you say to him?"

"Say to him? Like I said, I was kinda scared. At first I didn't say anything. Part of me was thinking I should just hang up, go up to my room, listen to some music, just walk away."

"Why didn't you?"

"I don't know why, I just didn't."

"Who spoke next?"

"He did."

"What did he say?"

"He said, 'Do you know who I am?'"

"Did you?"

"Not then, so I said no, but just as the word was coming out of my mouth, I knew who it was. I don't know how or why, but I knew it was him even though I couldn't remember if I'd ever heard his name before."

Bragg leans forward, putting his hand on his chin. "What did he say next?"

I let out this long sigh. It's like I've been holding my breath or something. "I told you what he said. I don't see why we have to keep going over and over this."

"Because each time you tell me, you give up more details. This is the last time, I promise. What did he say next?"

"Say? He didn't say anything at first; he just burst out crying. Crying like I've never heard a man cry before. This deep, rattling cry that seemed to just go on forever."

"Billy, what did you do when he was crying? How did you feel?"

"I started to cry too. I don't know why. I don't know what I was feeling. I just started to cry, and it seemed to make him cry harder, so I tried to stop but it was hard."

"Did he say anything when he was crying?"

"He tried to. He would start, stop, start, stop. Finally he managed to say, 'I'm . . . the . . . truck driver. I'm . . . the man who killed your father. I'm so sorry.' Then he kept saying, 'I'm sorry,' over and over again."

Bragg turns a page in his notebook and says, "Now try to remember what you did and said next, okay?"

"Well, like I said before, this is where it gets a little fuzzy. I listened to him cry for a while, but it was like I wasn't all there anymore. Almost like part of me had just walked away, leaving this shell standing in the kitchen with a phone held against his ear. I remember looking at this advertisement stuck on the refrigerator, a two-for-one sale for large pizzas at Sal's. I didn't know what to feel, I didn't know what to think.

"Finally I said the one thing I really did know that I felt. My voice seemed dull, almost like I was talking from the bottom of a drum. I said, 'What do you want?'"

"What did he say?"

"I'm still not sure. I think he said, 'I just wanted to say I'm sorry.' But like I said, I'm not sure."

"Now, this is where you lost your temper?"

"Yes."

"Do you remember what you said?"

"Yes, it just kind of came out. I said . . . 'I hope you die and I hope you go to hell.'"

The screen door slams and I'm off, running across our front yard. I hold my backpack under my arm like a twenty-pound football. You would think that after three weeks I'd be able to get this whole bus stop routine down like other people. You know, walk to the stop, talk to your friends while you wait, casually board the bus. Not me, I'm the crazed kid racing for the bus every morning. I'm the kid crashing through hedges, falling into holes, and hopping fences. I'm the kid huffing and puffing down the bus aisle every morning. It wasn't like this last year; why can't I seem to get it together this year?

I get the feeling that the bus driver doesn't really like me. I'm sure that if I get there just one second after the door closes, he's gone. I know this by the way he looks at me every morning; he glares at me. I'm fairly sure he speeds up a bit when he sees me running. I'm not totally positive, but I bet he's trying to prove a point. I think he finds my last-minute dash to the bus stop to be some kind of a character flaw. Maybe he believes that if I miss the bus a couple times, it will do me some good, build some of this lacking character. Either that or he thinks of it as some kind of a grand race. Who knows, maybe I'm the highlight of his pathetic morning.

Things are not looking good today. Now I'm positive that the driver thinks of me more as his competitor than his passenger. I know he's driving faster today. To save time, I crash through the neighbor's hedges instead of going around them. I run maybe fifteen feet before noticing a tepee of ropes spread out from a tree in front of me. Mrs. Kirshner must have had some work done on a few of the little trees in her front yard. They tied these ropes around them and staked the ropes to the ground. I guess to make them grow straighter. I jump the first stake but totally miss the second one. I go down hard and make this weird grunting sound when I hit the ground. My books spill out of my backpack like a dropped deck of playing cards. I just lie there for a second looking at all my books scattered around me. I'm thinking about giving up today, then I hear that bus again; I jump to my feet, cramming the books into my backpack. No, I will not let him beat me today. I'm off and running as fast as I can. I cut through another yard. The bus is at the stop; the line of kids is growing shorter. I make it just as the door is about to shut. The closest I've come to missing the morning bus all year. The driver shakes his head and snickers. I'm beginning to hate this guy.

Amy gives me a little wave; she's saved me a seat again. I'm having a real hard time catching my breath. I even feel dizzy. Some girl gives me one of those looks of revulsion that girls can do so well. Guys will normally say something to get under your skin; girls, well, they're way beyond that. They can rip your heart out with just a raised eyebrow. Today I don't hold it against her. I'm wheezing, sweating, and dirty, and great, I've also torn the knee of my pants. Oh, add bleeding to the list, mustn't forget bleeding; I've cut my left palm.

I flop down next to Amy. I try to straighten out the books in my backpack before they all fall out. What a mess. It looks like it was packed by a drunken monkey.

I turn to Amy and try to talk and catch my breath at the same time. "That guy . . ." Gasp. "Really seems . . ." Gasp. "To hate . . ." Gasp. "Me."

"Who?"

Gasp. "Bus driver."

She gives me this puzzled look. "Why do you think the bus driver hates you?"

Gasp. "By the way he seems to speed up when I run to the bus . . ." Gasp. "He wants me to miss it."

"Why don't you just get to the bus stop on time? Then

you won't have to make this mad dash every morning like an escaping mental patient. Do you need a new alarm clock? I think we have an extra."

"Yeah, yeah. I know, you're right. I don't know what's wrong with me. I just don't seem . . ." Gasp. "To be organized this year."

"Seriously, do you need an alarm clock? Because I'm sure we have an extra."

"No . . . uh, thanks, but no thanks. I've got one. It just seems like with the twins and everything, I just run out of time in the mornings."

"So, get up earlier."

"Yeah, yeah, you're right. I know you're right. I think I'll give myself an extra half hour tomorrow."

"Sounds like a good idea. Oh, I was thinking, you always say 'the twins'—do they have real names, or what?"

I laugh. "You know, you're right. Their names are Sara and Silvia."

"Cute names. They identical?"

"Yeah, sure are. They're as cute as their names, too. Well, you know what I mean."

Amy looks down and notices my hand. "Hey, your hand."

"Oh, it's nothing."

I finish organizing my books, zip up the bag, and place it on the floor.

"No, really, let me see. It's bleeding." She turns my hand and looks at it. "We should clean that up a bit. It could get infected."

Amy reaches into her handbag and takes out a couple of baby wipes. "I was babysitting last weekend. These things come in handy. Oh, and if you don't mind Mickey Mouse, I've got a couple of Band-Aids, too."

"Mickey Mouse is fine. Should go over well in gym class too."

She giggles, then reaches out, takes my hand, and starts to wipe the cut. Everything suddenly disappears. The bus, the other kids, the talking, the yelling, the driver's radio, the sun, the day, everything. All that's left in the world is my hand in Amy's. She's holding my hand. Her hand feels so delicate, so small, so different, so good. She's slowly, carefully wiping my cut. Each second, each moment, seems complete. I want them all to stretch, twist, and blend on forever. Stop, Time, please stop. Let me catch this feeling, let it be mine to explore, over and over again. It's too perfect to pass quickly.

I steal a quick look at her face: Her eyes are focused on my hand, she's lightly biting on her lower lip; her hair is flowing across her cheek. I wonder if she realizes how beautiful she is.

Still holding my hand, she applies two cartoon bandages and smoothes them out.

When she speaks, I realize we've been silent. We haven't spoken a word since she took my hand. "Billy, I want to ask you something. I've been meaning to ask you for a few days now but never got the chance, or maybe I just couldn't find the nerve."

"What?"

"Well . . . um . . ."

I look up from our hands and into her eyes. She seems nervous. Did I do something wrong? Is she mad at me?

"I've been meaning to ask you. Um, in two weeks there's going be that dance. You know, the Sadie Hawkins Dance? That's the one where the girl's supposed to ask the guy. You know? I was kind of wondering, if you're not busy or anything, would you like to go . . . with, you know . . . me?"

"You're asking *me* to the dance?"

"Yes."

"*Me?*"

"Yes."

"Really?"

"Yes, really. Do you want to go or don't you?"

I can't believe this is happening. Amy is so beautiful and so sweet. I wonder if I look as shocked as I feel. A girl is actually asking me out. Me. I can't believe it. She's looking at me. Answer her question, you idiot. "Well, yeah, I'd love to go with you. I don't drive, though, you know."

"I kind of figured that out."

"Yeah, right. Well, I guess we can figure out the whole driving thing later, huh?"

She gives my hand a little squeeze. "Hey, there's only two ways, really: We drive together with one of our parents, or we meet at the dance."

I can't believe we're talking about the details. The details of something make it real. Isn't that right? A plan without details is just an idea. It's like one of those paint-by-number pictures. It's just a bunch of numbers spread around on a piece of canvas. It's when you start matching the colors with the numbers and actually start filling it all in that it turns into something special. What's going to go wrong? That's what I want to know. This moment's perfect. What if the future doesn't work out—will this moment then become less than perfect?

Amy's giving me a strange look. "Is something wrong?"

"No, why?"

"You just looked kinda, well, I don't know."

"No, really, I'm fine."

I don't want to lose Amy as a friend. I'd love to go to the dance with her, and do other stuff with her, but not if it ruins our friendship. What if we go out a few times and it doesn't work out? Will we still sit together on the bus or talk together in the halls?

Suddenly Miss Gate pops into my head. Didn't she want me to go to the poetry-coffee-shop thing a week from

Friday? I'm sure of it. We've been going over my poems before homeroom for a few days now.

"I just thought of something."

"What?"

"I'm supposed to do something with my English teacher that night."

"What?"

"She's taking me to this poetry-type workshop that she belongs to."

"You'd rather do that?"

"No, um, of course not, it's just that I told her I would."

Amy looks like she's starting to get pissed. So I blurt out, "Listen, I'll try to get out of it, if I can. Okay? But I don't know. I'll have to see."

"Don't do anything you don't want to do."

"It's not that. I want to go with you. It's just, well, I don't know. I've got to talk to my teacher. Okay?"

Amy turns, looks out the window, and mutters, "Whatever."

This food is terrible. I mean, even by school lunch standards it's bad. It's spaghetti. How do you mess up spaghetti? It tastes like vinegar. I pick at it with my fork until I realize they dumped the spaghetti on top of my salad. Can't we have a separate bowl for the salad? Why put the two of them together? I take my milk and pudding and push the rest of the tray away.

"You gonna eat that?"

It's Chris Dalton. As far as I can tell, he's always hungry, and it shows. We're not really friends, we just always sit together during lunch. I'm not sure why.

"No."

"Can I have it?"

I push the tray over to him and he attacks it. The vinegar doesn't seem to bother him.

Ziggy plops down in the seat next to me, takes out his

iPod earbuds, and gives me a big slap on the back. "Dude! What's goin' on?"

He's the only guy I know who calls anyone "dude," but for some reason he can get away with it.

"Zig, what are you doing here? I thought you had B lunch."

"I do. I'm on my way to see my dad. He wants to talk to me about something, but I have to talk to ya first."

Ziggy's dad is one of the school guidance counselors. As far as guidance counselors go, everyone agrees he's one of the good guys.

"What's up?"

"Amy told me you don't want to go to that dance with her. What's up with that? I just talked to her for a second, but she seems really cool. Why don't you want to go with her?"

"How do you know Amy?"

He grins. "Well, she's a friend of Julie's, you know, Heather's friend."

"Who's Heather?"

"Oh, Heather is Mary's friend."

I try to remember Mary, but I come up blank. "Who's Mary?"

Ziggy rolls his eyes a bit and shakes his head. "Mary is Jen's best friend. You know, they're always together."

"Jen . . . your sister Jen?"

"Now you're on the right page."

"So, Jen knows Mary, who knows Heather, who knows . . . oh, forget about it. Just tell me what Amy said."

Ziggy shakes his head again. "All she really wants to know is why you don't want to go to the dance with her. I don't really get it either. Like I said, she seems nice."

Chris leans across the table. "Hey, you gonna eat your pudding?"

I shove it toward him and it almost falls into his lap.

"Zig, I told her. I want to go, I really do, but I have something I've gotta do with my English teacher that night. There's this . . . writing-type workshop that meets Friday nights, and she wants me to go with her that night."

Ziggy runs his fingers through his shaggy hair. "Hey, don't get me wrong. Your English teacher is hot, and I mean really hot, but Amy seems to like you big-time."

He leans in close to me and lowers his voice. "I know Amy really wants to go to the dance with you. The workshop meets every Friday night. Can't you go a different week?"

I hesitate for a moment but then figure, why not? "I guess I could move it, but I'm worried that this might not be the right time to go with Amy."

"Not the right time? It might be your only time."

"Zig, I really like Amy, but I'm not like you. I haven't been out with many girls before." Ziggy raises an eyebrow. "All right, I haven't been out with *any* girls before. She's the first girl I've ever really been able to talk to. I really enjoy being around her. What if it doesn't work out? What if we go out a couple times and she decides she doesn't like me? Then what? Then I lose her as a friend, too."

Ziggy lets out a long sigh. "Amy asked you out. Your relationship has changed. If you say no, there's a real good chance you're going to lose her friendship. You know what I mean? If you want things to work out, the odds are *way* better if you go with her to the dance. Girls tend to deal with rejection badly. Think about it. Don't end your friendship with her before it even has a chance to start."

Ziggy stands up. "Listen, just think about it, okay? I really have to fly—my dad's waiting. Who knows what he wants me to do now. I really hope he doesn't want me to show another new kid around the school. I'm just not in the mood to do that right now."

He starts to walk away but stops, comes back, and squats next to me. "Really, don't let Amy slip away. I can tell you two really like each other."

He slaps me on the back and starts to walk away again.

"Later, Zig . . . and Zig?"

He stops and turns toward me.

"Thanks."

He gives me this huge smile. "Hey, no problem. We're buds, we stick together, ain't that right?"

I'm standing at the open door watching her: She's bent over her desk in the empty classroom. The lights are on but it feels dark. I'm about to knock, but for some reason I stop and watch her instead. I thought she was working on something, but I realize she's crying. Why is she crying? Maybe it's best if she doesn't see me. I'll stop by later. I start to walk away.

"Billy?"

I turn to her; she's quickly wiping her eyes with a tissue. "Yes, Miss Gate?"

"Did you want something?"

"Nothing important. I'll come back later."

"No, it's okay, come on in."

I walk across the room and sit at the chair next to her desk. She continues to wipe her eyes. We sit together in silence; it's weird that she doesn't say anything, so after a while I ask, "Something wrong, Miss Gate?"

"Tess."

"Something wrong, Tess?"

"No, I'm fine. I just get . . . sad sometimes. I don't know why. It just kind of . . ." She shakes her head and leaves the thought unfinished.

"Just kind of . . . washes over you like a wave?"

Her head snaps up. "Yes, Billy, that's it exactly, like a wave. The sadness washes over me like a wave."

"I know what that's like. It happens to me a lot about my father. I'll be doing something, talking to a friend, doing my homework, something like that, and out of nowhere the sadness washes over me and I just start thinking about my dad."

"I'm sorry to hear that, but you're right, that's what it's like for me."

"Is it about your father too?"

"My father?" She pauses. "Oh, no. Sometimes, maybe, but mainly it's just . . . things."

Tess wipes her eyes again, and I guess I should try to change the subject, but I can't seem to let it go. "What kinds of things?"

She manages to give me a slight smile. "Billy, that's one of the things I like about you. You're very inquisitive; it's quite endearing."

Tess stares out the window; she seems lost in thought. "What kinds of things? All kinds of things. Regrets seem to plague me the most. I guess it's one of the curses of being an adult. When you're growing up, you paint this picture in your mind of what it's going to be like when you're older. You think that the career and the independence will bring you a rewarding happiness, but it doesn't seem to work out that way."

She leans back in her chair, runs her hands through her hair, tilts her head backward, and shakes it free. Her breasts seem to strain against her tight shirt like separate living creatures. Then she produces a rubber-band-type thing and ties her hair behind her head.

"I always wanted to be a teacher, as far back as I can remember. I thought that once I got my degree and was teaching, all of the other things in my life would line up like dominoes. . . . God no, not dominoes, like ducks, yes, ducks, I hoped everything would line up like ducks and I'd be happy, but it's not happening. I feel just as empty as I've ever felt. To make matters worse, now I find myself regretting all the things I didn't do when I was young. Oh, I don't know . . . ."

She turns and stares out the window again. This is all so strange. I look at my shoelaces; I almost wish they were untied just to give me something to do. Why didn't I just walk away before, when I had a chance? I should say something, but I don't know what to say. Bragg would try to say something clever to make her feel better, but I'm not

Bragg. I remember the ducks that used to live in the pond behind our house.

"Tess, I wouldn't waste too much time waiting for ducks to line up; they're really stupid birds."

She laughs and smiles. "Oh, I love you. You're great. You say the most incredible things."

"Uh . . . thanks." Did she say 'I love you'?

Tess seems to gain some control of herself. "I'm sorry, Billy. Did you want to talk to me about something?"

"Yeah, I did, but we can talk later if you want."

"No, it's okay. What did you want to talk about?"

Suddenly I'm a bit nervous. I don't want to upset her again, but it's kind of pointless not to talk about it now. Besides, why would she be upset? "It's about the poetry reading in two weeks. Do you think we could do it another night?"

"Another night? Why?"

"Well, um, something came up and I can't do it that night."

She's looking at me, but I can't seem to figure out what she's thinking. "Sure, I guess we could do it another night. Is everything okay?"

"Yeah, everything's fine." I hesitate. Should I tell her? Why wouldn't I tell her? "It's just that I got asked to the Sadie Hawkins Dance."

Tess looks at me. She doesn't say a word. Maybe she doesn't know what the Sadie Hawkins Dance is. But I'm sure she must have seen the posters around the school. I could be wrong, but I think this Sadie Hawkins Dance thing was around when she was in school. Why is she looking at me like this? It's the same look you see in cop shows when they're interrogating some worthless criminal in a small back room with a bright light. That look they give them right before they slam their hand on the desk and start shouting. Suddenly the look changes, maybe it wasn't even there, and she gives me a huge smile. "Billy, that's great news. I didn't know you had a girlfriend."

"Well, Amy's not my girlfriend. We just kinda talk and stuff like that."

"Oh, so her name is Amy? What's her last name? Is she in one of my classes?"

"It's Amy Wilson, and no, she has Mrs. Bleaker for English."

Tess keeps smiling. "Oh, that's so nice. I'm very happy for you." But she doesn't look happy, even though she's smiling. "So then you're definitely not going to be able to make the poetry night, right?"

"I guess not, at least not that night. Like I said, I think we could do it another night."

She gathers the papers on her desk and starts to stack them all in a neat pile. It seems like she's starting to get mad for some reason. "Guess what? That date worked well with my schedule. Do you expect me to keep all of *my*

Friday nights open to accommodate *your* schedule?"

"No, of course not. I'm sorry. I . . . I just thought we could work something else out."

She lets out a long sigh and just stares at me for a while. I don't understand why she seems to be getting so mad at me. I should have talked about all this later. I guess now wasn't the right time. Finally she blurts out, "I'm sure we can work something out, but I don't want to have to keep constantly changing my schedule around. You know, I have things I like to do too."

"Well, yeah, of course you do. I'm sorry."

Tess leans over and picks through her pocketbook on the floor; I can see right down her shirt. She finds her calendar and starts to flip quickly through the pages. I can see most of her breasts. "How about this Friday? Will this Friday work for you?"

I can't believe I just saw her breasts. Her breasts! I hope she didn't see me looking down her shirt. That would be really embarrassing, but I couldn't help myself. It's not like I had planned to look down her shirt. It just happened. She leaned over and—*bam!*—there they were. It's like when you're channel surfing and you come across some baseball game and the pitcher is throwing the ball: You just have to wait a second to see if the batter's going to hit it. It's almost like you don't have a choice.

"Well? Will this Friday work for you or not?"

Friday? Oh yeah, poetry reading, focus on her question. Stop thinking about her breasts. I don't want her to be mad at me anymore. Let's see, Friday. Oh God, Friday's only four days away. Four days! I'd like to say "No, let's do it another time; it's too soon." I have a ton of excuses running through my head, and any one of them would probably work, but instead I open my mouth and hear myself saying, "Yeah, sure, um, this Friday will be fine."

I close the door behind me and I'm standing in the empty, locker-lined corridor. It stretches out before me. I begin to walk toward my next class. The boxed fluorescent lights pass over me. My sneakers squeak, my legs feel weak, my backpack bites into my shoulder. The empty hall reminds me of a mine shaft.

When I was about eight, I remember watching my neighbor Mr. Foster going to work one morning. He lived across the street on top of the hill. One morning he drove his BMW about three quarters of the way down the driveway, stopped the car, got out, and walked about ten feet to pick up his newspaper. The car made this popping sound; I guess it was the e brake. It moved slowly for a few feet before it picked up speed and raced down the rest of the driveway. It sailed across the street and down our front yard, missing our house by inches before crashing loudly in our backyard. The car was totaled.

What I remember most about that morning is the way

Mr. Foster just stood and watched his car roll away. I never understood why he didn't at least try to catch it. If he had moved quickly right at the beginning, he would have had a chance, but instead he hesitated, and that hesitation cost him his car.

I don't want to read a poem Friday night. I'm not even sure I'll be ready to read a poem Friday night. I should have said something to Tess. I should have asked for more time, or better yet, just told her that I've changed my mind, that I don't want to read in front of a room full of strangers. But like Mr. Foster, I hesitated. I stood by and watched my chance roll away.

It's taken me five years to understand why Mr. Foster didn't run for his car. I wonder what I'll understand five years from now.

After my next class I run down to Amy's locker, hoping to catch her. I want to tell her about the dance and how much I really want to go with her. I can't let another chance roll away. I'm in luck. I can see her spinning the combination lock with a strange, faraway look in her eyes. The halls are crowded and she doesn't seem to notice me.

For some reason I decide to sneak up behind her. I surprise her by quickly reaching out and giving her sides a little tickle while calling out, "Blaaa!"

She lets out a short, high-pitched squeal. Her knee jerks

up and slams into the locker. She drops her books, clutches her knee, and howls in pain.

"Amy, I'm sorry! Are you okay?"

"Billy!" She glares at me. "What's wrong with you? Why did you do that?"

"I'm sorry. I'm sorry. I didn't think you'd jump like that."

She snaps, "Well, what did you expect me to do?"

"I don't know what I was thinking. I'm sorry. Are you okay?"

She's rubbing her knee. "Yeah, I guess."

I pick up her books and hand them to her. This isn't the way I planned on telling Amy about the dance. Why did I do that?

"Sorry, I just wanted to surprise you . . . that's all."

"Congratulations. You surprised me."

"Actually, what I wanted to do was tell you something."

"You mean besides . . . 'Blaaa!'?"

"What? Oh yeah, sorry."

She starts to bend her knee back and forth.

"Are you sure you're okay?"

"Yes, I'm fine. What did you want to tell me?"

"Oh, just that I got out of the poetry thing and I can go to the dance with you."

"You got out of it?"

"Yeah, no problem."

"I thought it *was* a problem."

"It wasn't a problem. Really."

"Are you sure you want to go? Because I don't want you to go with me if you're not completely sure."

I look her in the eye. "Yeah, I'm completely sure. I really want to go with you."

"Was messing up my knee part of your master plan?"

"Does it hurt?"

She smiles. "Nah, I'm just giving you a hard time."

"Okay, but I really am sorry. Um . . ."

I look at her and I want to say something smart or funny, something that would make me seem cool and intelligent, but nothing pops into my head. The silence is becoming painful. I desperately claw for words but can't find any. I hope it's not going to be like this at the dance. "Well, I've got to, you know . . . run now. I've got to get all the way over to science lab."

Her eyes brighten and a little smile forms on her face. "I'm glad at least one of us can run. I'm going to limp on down to the library."

Dear Dad,

I know this sounds strange, but sometimes I stare at myself in the bathroom mirror. I mean, not just for a minute or two, but for a really, really long time. That's a bit weird, isn't it? I just stand there with the door locked. I stand and stare and wonder. I look deep into my eyes, almost like I'm looking for something. I look at my nose, my ears, my mouth, the shape of my head. I'm searching for something. Something I don't understand. It's like this person I'm looking at isn't really me. When I sleep and I dream, I'm not this person looking back at me. I know that sounds strange, but I think it's true; at least, that's how it feels.

I wonder if other people do this. Did you? Is it just another one of those things that everyone does but no one admits to? At night when I'm staring into the mirror, are some of my neighbors doing the very same thing? At any given moment are there millions of people across the world standing in front of mirrors, searching for something?

What does it mean? Am I the only person feeling this way? I guess I could be. I remember when we all used to go to church together. I'd sit in the same pew with a bunch of other people, and it always seemed to me that even though we were all watching the same service, from the same place, we were all having totally different experiences.

What about reincarnation? If there is such a thing as reincarnation, could that mean that you're back here someplace? Could you be someone's little baby? Could you be sleeping soundly in a crib right now, covered in a warm, comfortable blanket, with loving parents standing by waiting to grant you your every wish and desire? I really like that idea. I might like that idea more than the idea of heaven, but I'm not sure.

Dad, I'm thinking too much. I'm feeling too much. I want to turn it off. I want my brain to just shut down for a while. I don't want to miss you this much. I don't want to feel like there's a big hole in my chest or that I'm just this little feather in front of a huge fan. Why can't I just push it all behind me or at least walk over it? Why can't I grow stronger? Nobody seems to know how weak I feel. I

don't want to spend so much time thinking about how I let
you down that morning. Think this, think that, think, think,
think. You have no idea how it just wears you down. I feel
like this little pony pulling a huge cart of heavy junk through
the mud. I don't think I'm big enough to pull this cart. I
don't understand it all; is the present more about the past or
the future? The present seems like a giant puzzle to me. The
future seems so far away from me right now that I can't
even pretend to know what it's going to be like. All I seem to
have right now is the past, and it's nothing more than this
nasty bully who seems to love to kick me around every day.

Sometimes it makes me angry. I know it's wrong to be
angry, but I can't help it. It's like every bone in my life
was broken. Why did this happen? Why did it happen to
us? Why you? Why me? Why Mom? Why the twins? Will
they even remember you when they grow up? I want to hit
someone or hate something. I'd rather destroy everything
around me, rip everything to pieces, than have all this
destroy Mom, me, or the twins. I miss myself; I don't like
this new self that your death created.

I hate the truck driver who killed you. I hate him,
I really do. I'd like to somehow hurt him as much as he's
hurt me, but I can't even imagine what I'd have to do to

do that. I know it's not right, but I can't help the way I feel. He called me to say he was sorry. I told him to go to hell. I should have just hung up. Hell can't put anything back together again.

Did God take you away from me? If so, why? Does God hate me? I look at so many kids with their dads and I think: Why didn't God take his dad instead of mine? I know that sounds bad, but don't I have the right to ask that question? I think I own that question. I really do. It's my question, I didn't ask for it, it was pushed upon me, and if I choose to use it every time I see someone evil, violent, or self-centered, I think that's my right. Why you and not this or that person? Why you and not someone who's part of all the things that are wrong with the world? If there's a God, wouldn't it make more sense for him to take away the bad and leave the good? I don't think God's playing fair. Please, Dad, don't play fair either. Fight God; come back to me. I know that's a stupid thing to say, but it makes me feel better just to say it.

Bragg tells me it's normal to be angry. He even says it's "healthy." He says it's part of the whole grieving process. I wonder how "healthy" he would think it was if he only knew what I was thinking. I was thinking of grabbing this stupid statue that he has on the coffee table and smacking him over the head with it. Would that be healthy? I doubt it, but maybe it would shut him up for a while, and that's got to be worth something.

"Five, four, three, two, one . . . Ready or not, here I come!" I uncover my face and look around the room. Sara pops her head down behind a chair, while Silvia stands behind the fish tank. I pretend I don't see them. I walk around the room, mumbling, "Gee, where are the twins? Where could they be hiding?" I quickly open closet doors and look under the couch and table. I scratch my head a lot, fail to notice them, and continue to make a huge show of looking in all the wrong places.

After a few minutes a little voice calls out, "We're over here!"

I pretend I can't tell where the voice is coming from and head off in the wrong direction.

"No, we're over here!"

I put my hand to my ear. "Gee, where's that voice coming from? It sounded like the kitchen." I move in that direction.

Now both voices call out, "No, we're in the living room!"

"The living room? That can't be right. I looked all over the living room."

"Look behind the chair!"

"And behind the fish tank!"

I scratch my head again. "Gee, behind the chair and fish tank? What great hiding places. Maybe it's a trick."

I hear giggling. "No, it's not a trick!"

I run into the living room and "find" Sara squatting down behind the chair, then quickly "find" Silvia. I shout out "Aha!" both times, then pump my fists in the air before beating them on my chest and loudly proclaiming, "Yes, I am the greatest hide-and-seeker of all time! No one is better. I am the greatest! The greatest, I tell you! Nobody can hide from Billy the Great!"

The girls giggle even louder.

I continue to thump my chest and shout, "I am the greatest!" The girls are now laughing loudly.

The doorbell rings.

I take off running. The girls follow. We're still laughing as we quickly move through the house. We're all in our stocking feet. When I get close to the front door, I slide the last ten feet on the hardwood floor.

I look through the peephole and I'm surprised to see Miss Gate out there. She's all crooked, elbows and knees bent in strange directions; she seems to be struggling with her pocketbook, some books, and a compact mirror. She's holding all three but mainly seems to be focused on the mirror, patting and fluffing her hair while balancing her pocketbook on her knee. Her short skirt keeps blowing around in the breeze. It's kinda fun to watch, until the twins grow impatient and spoil the moment with their questions.

I open the door.

"Hi, Miss Gate. What are you doing here?"

She slips the compact back into her pocketbook and straightens her stack of books. "I've got a little extra time. I thought, if you'd like, we could work together a bit on your poems. You said you were nervous about the reading. Maybe we should work on them. Smooth out any rough edges."

"Um, I'm babysitting tonight. My mother's out, some-thing with work, she told me, but I wasn't really paying attention. She'll be out for a couple of hours."

Tess raises an eyebrow. "Billy, she's hosting that real estate seminar at the school, remember?"

"Oh yeah, that's right. It's a big deal for her. I told her not to worry about a thing, I'd watch the twins tonight."

"I'm sure she wouldn't mind me stopping by. Right? When I babysat in high school, I used to study with friends all the time. You get to study, and the parents get four eyes watching their kids instead of two. Besides, with me you get a highly trained professional as your second pair of eyes."

She smiles at Sara and Silvia, who immediately beam huge smiles right back at her. The twins love the attention of any and all females. I suspect it's some kind of unspoken lifetime membership given to girls at birth. I've noticed the way girls of any age always gather in groups and speak in hushed or coded words. It's definitely some kind of secret club with rules, dress codes, and a different type of language that involves body and face movement. My dad told me about it. He said it's nearly impossible for guys to break the code; it's best to nod your head a lot and pretend you know what's going on. It seems like good advice.

Once when we were hanging a shelf together, Dad said, "If you only remember one thing I tell you, remember this: Right to tighten, left to loosen." I think he was just joking. I have to admit, though, I do use the "Right to tighten" thing a lot, so who knows. Maybe the things in life that don't make much sense to me don't really make sense to anyone. Maybe what my dad was really saying is, "I can show you how to put up a shelf, but there's a whole lot in this life you're going to have to try to figure out yourself." Or like I said, maybe it was just a joke. I guess I'll never know now.

Tess reaches out and pats Sara on the head. "Hello, and what is your name?"

Sara and Silvia suddenly become shy and move behind my legs, but I can tell they're still very interested in Tess.

Finally Silvia looks around me and says, "Her name's Sara, and I'm Silvia. Who are you?"

"I'm your brother's English teacher. You can call me Tess. You two are so cute."

Sara looks around my other leg. "Thank you."

"Your brother's told me so much about you two. Guess what? I brought you something."

Suddenly the twins aren't shy anymore, and they both shout, "You did! What? What did you bring?"

Tess reaches into her pocketbook and hands Sara a DVD. She grabs it and squeals, "*The Wiggles!* We love *The Wiggles!*"

After I get the twins set up in the living room with *The Wiggles*, I join Tess at the kitchen table. I sit next to her on the bench. She has two books of poetry spread out, a note-pad, pens, and about a half dozen of my poems.

"Oh my God, if I have to read six poems in front of a group of people, I will pass out. I'm not joking. They'll be picking me up off the floor."

"Stop it, Billy. You're not going to read six poems. I just thought we'd go over these together and figure out which one is best. That's all."

"You think those are my best? Which ones?"

Tess smiles and shakes her head. "I don't believe you."

"What? What don't you believe?"

"You try to act like your poems aren't that important to you, but it's obvious that they are."

I move the poems around. "Well, I did take the time to write them. If they had no importance, I doubt I'd do that. . . . So you like these the best?"

"I like these the best, but I'm not sure these *are* the best. You have a lot of great poems. All poems have different voices that speak to people differently. These six happen to speak to me."

I push them around the table a bit more. "So which one 'speaks' to you the loudest?"

Tess thinks for a moment before moving one forward. "I think this one, 'Sweet with the Sour.'"

I shrug. "Okay, then let's work on that one."

For the next hour Tess and I go over the poem. Line by line, word by word. I've never worked on a poem this way before. Tess keeps stressing that every word has to be the perfect word, every sentence the perfect sentence. At first it seems like a pain, but then I get what she means and it becomes very exciting.

We work well together as we take sentences apart and put them back together again. Replacing words, adding lines. As we work, we keep leaning closer and closer together; I don't realize how close until I feel Tess's leg and hip pressed up against mine. Once I become aware of it, that's all I can feel. It's like every sense of feeling in my body has migrated south to my leg. Her leg doesn't move and my leg doesn't move; they just press up against each other. It's almost as if our legs are dancing the slowest slow dance ever, a dance of complete stillness.

As we continue to work, I become more aware of the things I didn't notice before: the sound of her breathing, the fresh smell of her shampoo, every slight touch of her shoulder, her elbow, her hand. For some reason my mind rushes back to the other day at school, when Tess leaned down to go through her pocketbook and I could see down her shirt. I've thought about that brief three or four seconds more than I'd ever want to admit. How can three clicks of the second hand wind up taking up so much of my time?

I'm breathing funny, somehow harder, deeper. She's going to notice and wonder what I'm thinking about. I try to control myself. I try smaller breaths, but then I feel like a puppy. I try waiting longer between breaths, but then I feel like I'm gasping. Finally I try matching Tess's breathing. This works fine for a little while, but then something strange starts to happen. It's like we become one person. Everything becomes about the breathing, all I can hear is the breathing. All the other noises in the house fade away. I just hear my breathing and Tess's. It seems like we're both breathing harder. Breathe in, breathe out, breathe in, breathe out. I feel locked in. We're not working anymore. When did we stop?

The house begins to rumble, the floor shakes. Dad

never had the time to replace the old electric garage-door opener.

The twins run through the kitchen, heading toward the back door, shouting, "Mommy's home! Mommy's home!"

Tess's head snaps up. "Oh my God! It's so loud. I thought the whole house was falling down or we were having an earthquake or something."

I can't help smiling, not a normal smile, but one of those huge, goofy ones that stretch your face all out of shape. "Yeah, we've gotta get that thing fixed."

She starts gathering the books and papers. "I think we made some excellent progress tonight. What do you think?"

I try to gather my thoughts. I hear my mother's car door close and her high heels tapping across the cement garage floor.

"Um . . . yeah, I guess." I'd like to say more, but I just can't seem to find the words.

My mother's slowly walking up the old wooden steps. Each step sounds dull and hollow, distant and close at the same time.

Sara opens the door and calls down to her. "Hello, Mommy."

"Hey, sweetheart. You having a good night?" She sounds tired.

"Yeah, Mommy, and guess what? Billy's teacher's here too."

"I thought that was her car."

Tess gently places her hand on my shoulder and looks me in the eye. "You did really good tonight. I mean it."

"Um . . . thank you, I guess."

Sara's telling my mother about hide-and-seek and the *Wiggles* DVD.

As my mother gets closer to the door, Tess slowly slides away from me. She's standing when my mother walks into the room. They greet each other with warm hellos. She helps my mother with a box she's carrying. The two of them talk together; they laugh; they seem to be connecting in some kind of strange, sisterly way.

I sit and watch the two of them talking. I can't stop looking at Tess. It's like drinking cold water on a hot summer's day. Was it really just a few minutes ago that she had her leg pressed up against mine? Were we really just inches apart, touching elbows, shoulders, and hands, breathing together in silence? Sinking together into that warm, quiet place I didn't understand? It feels like it was a dream.

Tess moves her hand up to her forehead, then slowly runs it through her golden hair. She glances my way and gives me the briefest of smiles, a smile unlike any I've ever received; it's like she's opened the night for a glimpse of the sun. It's just a flash, but something in that flash is enough to let me know that it really wasn't a dream.

Something happened.

"I hate these shoes. They make me feel like such a . . . dork."

Ziggy snaps back his head and raises an eyebrow. "Dude, did you say 'dork'? Nobody says 'dork.'"

I shake my head. "You know what? Nobody says 'dude,' either, so give me a break. I just hate these shoes, that's all."

"Everybody has to wear the shoes. You'd look like a 'dork' if you didn't wear them. But hey, what do you care about how you look? You're the one who picked out a pink bowling ball. Nobody's gonna notice your shoes with that ball in your hand."

I hold the ball and gently toss it up and down. "But it's the perfect weight. The others are all too light or too heavy; this one's just right."

"Dude, it's pink."

"It's not really pink; it's, you know, a light red."

Ziggy looks at me for a moment. "Fine, you want that

ball. What do I care? Just stop complaining about your shoes."

He sighs and shakes his head. "First it takes me forever to talk you out of your house, and now all you do is complain about the shoes. At least *try* to have a good time."

Speakers buried in the ceiling crackle to life. A deep, energetic voice booms, "Welcome to . . . Light the Night bowling! I hope you all got your games on. Just call me Hank, 'cause that's my name. Tonight I'll be spinning some tunes, commenting on the games, and, more important, giving out some cold, hard cash. Do you think you could use some extra cash? I bet you can! So don't forget to pay attention, and remember your lane numbers. Here's a little something to get you pumped up for the night!"

An old Eminem song suddenly blasts from the speakers. It's way too loud and everyone collectively jumps. Hank quickly tries to turn it down but mistakenly turns it up even higher. The speakers pop and scream like an advancing army of fingernails across a chalkboard battlefield. Finally the volume lowers to its proper level.

Ziggy and I look at each other and laugh.

We head over to our lane, number five. Ziggy places his ball on the rack, sits at the table, and starts to set up the score sheet. I place my ball next to Ziggy's and notice a black one left there from the previous game. I pick it up and it seems just a little heavier than my pink one.

"Hey, Zig, this ball's perfect!" It's not really, but at least it's not pink.

He gives me a thumbs-up. "Does this mean you're going to start complaining about the shoes again?"

"I still think the shoes look dorky."

"Dorky, huh?"

I sit down next to Ziggy. "You want to take a couple practice rolls? It's been a while since I bowled."

"Nah, why don't we wait? I've got a couple friends joining us. If you don't have at least four per lane, they just randomly team you up with somebody. Last time that happened to me it was a total disaster. This Wednesday Light the Night thing is really popular."

"It is?"

"Yeah, it's kinda fun. You'll see. Hank is corny, but he's funny, and he really does give away a lot of cash."

"How much?"

"Oh, that depends. He sits up in that booth, watches the games, and yells out things like, 'The cute girl on four, roll a strike and I'll give you a five.' It just makes it more fun. Also, the music's not bad either."

I'm a little disappointed that someone's joining us. I thought it was just going to be the two of us. Ziggy didn't say anything about his friends when he called.

"So, who else is coming?"

He's busy setting up the score sheet, looking for the

overhead light switch, cleaning and moving everything around like some kind of Martha Stewart. "Oh, Julie Belle and one of her friends."

I can't believe this. Is he setting me up with someone? I'm not in the mood right now. I just wanted to go out and have some fun with Zig. Now I'll be spending the night struggling to say something clever. Or worse than that, what if this girl doesn't like me? What if I don't like her? What if we just sit and glare at each other all night? What if I do something really stupid? I don't want to spend the rest of the night desperately tangled in this "what if" spiderweb.

I shouldn't let Ziggy see that all this is freaking me out. I should at least try to act cool. Don't just sit here like a mushroom; say something.

"It feels like they waxed the inside of these shoes. My toes are slipping around."

"Billy, enough with the shoes, okay?"

"Ever wonder how many people have worn these things? I mean, how long can a pair of shoes last? At the very least a year, but maybe something like two or three. So at least a few hundred people have worn these shoes before, but it's possible that it could be as much as a thousand people. Think about it. A thousand people, a thousand pairs of smelly feet."

"Please, enough with the shoes already. My head's starting to hurt."

Maybe I am going on a bit too much about the shoes.

I watch Ziggy fill out the score sheet. He puts his name on the top, followed by Julie Belle's, then my name. He hesitates for a moment before writing "Amy Wilson" below my name.

"Amy Wilson's coming tonight? My Amy?"

Ziggy smiles. "I told you she was Julie's friend."

I'm suddenly even more nervous. I can actually feel my heart beating faster. My knees start to shake and my palms feel like they're getting sweaty. How do I look? Why did I wear this dumb shirt? Did I put on deodorant? What if I make a jerk out of myself tonight? I wish I had time to psych myself up. Get my head in the right place. Maybe think of a bunch of things to talk about, in case I can't think of anything.

Ziggy puts his arm around my shoulders and pulls me close. "Hey, we're buds, remember? We'll help each other out. Don't worry. It's going to be a great night. Just don't spend the whole time talking about your shoes."

His eyes open wide. "Julie! Amy! Over here!"

The two girls join us. Ziggy gives Julie a quick, awkward hug, then introduces me. I say, "Hello." I think about introducing him to Amy but realize they already know each other.

I smile at Amy. I manage to say, "Hey," and she says, "Hey," back to me.

Then we all just stand there with these forced, desperate smiles painted on our faces, trying to think of something, anything, to say.

I stick my hands in my pockets. I take them out. I stick them behind my back. I bounce on my toes. The suffocating silence starts to stretch on. This is terrible. I feel like screaming. Why isn't Ziggy saying something? I thought he was supposed to be so smooth with the ladies.

Finally he clears his throat. "I feel like such a dork in these shoes."

I laugh louder than I have in weeks. We all do. It's like we swam up together from a deep dive, broke to the surface at the same time, and gasped in that first breath of fresh air.

I walked in here tonight with no expectations and find myself having a fantastic time. Bowling, of all things. Who would have thought I'd have so much fun bowling? But I guess it's not the bowling that's making it so special. It's the people I'm with; they're true friends. It makes me realize that I've spent far too much time by myself. Just because someone doesn't understand what I'm going through doesn't mean they're not my friend. It just means that they don't understand.

The hands of the clock spin quickly. They don't creep or crawl, but fly. We laugh, talk, sing, and bowl away the spinning minute hand. The night moves quicker than any night in my life.

The speaker crackles. "Let's see. As the night is coming

to a close, we've got Billy on lane five going for the strike and the game. Sorry, buddy, you've had a good run, but ten bucks says you're not going to make it."

"Dude, don't listen to him. You can do it!"

Amy and Julie put their arms around each other and do a little cheerleader dance. They shout, "Go, Billy! Go, Billy! Go, go, go!"

I stand with the ball in my hands. I stare at the pins at the end of the lane like a gunslinger. I feel everybody looking at me. I can make this. I know I can. Maybe yesterday I would have had my doubts, but today I feel confident. I tell myself to try to move in one even, fluid motion, like when I gently pressed down the accelerator of Tess's Mustang. The memory brings back her face, her smile, her body, the feel of her leg pressed up against mine. I remember looking over at her when she drove, the top down, the wind whipping her hair around her face.

I run forward, swing my arm down, and release the ball. It moves fast, smooth, and straight before violently tumbling down all the pins. They don't hesitate or wobble; they just crash and scatter like bugs.

"Nice roll on five. Collect your ten!"

I turn around just in time to catch Amy as she leaps into my arms. She shouts, "Yeah! Nice roll!"

I look over her shoulder: Ziggy and Julie are smiling. Everybody looks so alive. I want this moment. I want to remember it always. I want to place it in a black box and pull it out whenever I'm feeling blue.

I hold Amy longer than I should, but she doesn't seem to mind. We look into each other's eyes. She has such beautiful eyes; they sparkle. I think about kissing her. Earlier tonight I placed my arm awkwardly around her shoulders while we were filling in the score sheet together. She didn't object; she seemed to like it. This might be a good time to kiss her. Not necessarily a big kiss. Just a little one on the lips. Maybe not the lips. The cheek? The neck?

I can feel her loosening her grip. I hesitate; it's Mr. Foster's runaway car all over again. I think I missed my chance to kiss her, but that's okay. At least I *almost* kissed her. When I awoke this morning, I had no idea that the end of the day would find me holding Amy in my arms, looking into her eyes, and thinking about kissing her.

Two years ago I almost jumped off a cliff into the water below, but I lost my nerve. But you know what? At least I had the courage to climb the cliff, to stand on its lip, to contemplate the jump. There are so many people who never find the courage even to climb the cliff.

Tonight I lost the nerve to kiss the girl, but at least I had the girl in my arms, at least I was able to see what that moment before a kiss feels like. One day next summer I'm sure I'll go down to the lake and jump off that cliff. One day soon I'll kiss the girl.

Mr. Knight pulls his Jeep Cherokee off the main road and onto our gravel driveway. His headlights catch a raccoon; its eyes glow like red lumps of hot coal. The animal bolts for the woods as we head down the hill. The rocks crunch under the tires.

Something about our house seems darker, somehow less inviting. I realize the outdoor lights are off. Mom normally leaves them on when I go out at night. I guess she forgot. I'm surprised how dark it is without them.

We stop outside the garage.

Ziggy starts to laugh.

"What's so funny?"

"Dude, I was thinking about you and that pink bowling ball again."

"I didn't use it."

"You were going to."

"But I didn't."

Ziggy's dad turns around. "Well, Billy, it was good to see you again."

"Yeah, you too, Mr. Knight. Thanks for the ride."

"No problem. Have you got your key?"

"Nah, we never lock the door. I guess we should, but we don't."

"Well, you really should. Times have changed, you know. Chris Dalton's house was robbed three weeks ago."

"Really? I sit with that guy every day at lunch, and all we ever talk about is who's going to eat my dessert. You'd think he'd mention something like getting robbed."

Ziggy starts to laugh, and his dad turns around and gives him a look that stops him instantly.

"Guys, I want you to be nice to Chris Dalton. He's going through some real tough times. I can't talk about it, but he could really use a friend right now, or at the very least just somebody he can talk to."

We're both surprised by the news and agree to be nicer to Chris. I shake Mr. Knight's hand and thank him again.

Ziggy holds out his fist and I lightly punch his knuckles.

"Later, dude."

"Later, Zig."

I stumble through the darkness before opening the back door and turning on the garage light. Moths appear from nowhere and start to circle it. Mr. Knight taps his horn a final good-bye as he heads out of our driveway.

I bound up the back stairs to the kitchen, and I'm about to call out to my mom, but I stop. Something feels wrong.

It's too dark. Normally at night all the lights are on. Now there's a small lamp that's on, but nothing else. That lamp's never on; I even forgot it was there.

I reach for the light switch but stop; instead I call out in a voice that's just a hair above normal talking range, "Mom?"

I slowly walk into the kitchen.

"Mom?"

I look around. There's a bunch of my mom's real estate flyers scattered about on the floor. There's an empty bottle of wine on the counter. My mother hardly ever drinks. Sometimes she would with Dad, but I haven't seen her have a drink in months. I'm scared. Something's wrong here. I can feel it. Is there someone in the house? Should I call 911?

I walk into the living room and quickly look around. Nothing seems to be missing. I grab the fireplace poker and head back into the kitchen. I'm not sure how much help it would be, but at least it makes me feel braver.

"Mom?"

I stand perfectly still in the middle of the kitchen, hold my breath, and listen, searching the house with my ears. I think I hear something coming from Dad's old office.

I walk to the hall. It's dark. At the other end of the hall

the office door is open a few inches. A slant of light stretches out from the door and runs toward me before marching up the wall and across the ceiling. I can hear faint music.

"Mom?"

I creep down the hall, poker in my hand. I feel like I'm climbing down a mine shaft. I walk on my toes. I try not to breathe.

The closer I get to the office, the clearer the music becomes. It's Dad's music. Bruce Springsteen. I grew up with the Boss. It's what my dad loved to listen to. Many a night I fell asleep with Springsteen playing downstairs, strange lullabies from a different time.

I reach out in the darkness and gently push open the office door. The light hurts my eyes. I inch into the room and look around. What? I don't understand.

A small voice escapes from my mouth before I can retrieve it. "Daddy?"

He's on the couch, wearing his brown leather jacket and Yankees cap.

The breath feels like it was pulled out of my chest. I can't breathe, I'm dizzy, and I can't seem to move; my feet suddenly feel like they've been disconnected from my body.

I sluggishly move toward the couch, dragging my feet. Springsteen is singing about diving into a river. The room feels like it's spinning; I'm getting so dizzy, I'm worried I'm about to fall.

"Dad?"

I can see the coffee table. There's photo albums and pictures of my dad scattered on it. There's half a glass of wine and a bunch of Springsteen CDs.

Am I dreaming? Am I falling?

I move around the couch.

I look at the jacket and the hat, but the face isn't my dad's. It's my mother's. She's wearing his jacket and hat. Her head is leaning to the side, her eyes are closed, and she's sleeping.

I stand and look at her for a while. Springsteen plays on. I wonder if I should wake her. Maybe it's best if I just let her sleep.

I walk over to the stereo, lean the fireplace poker against the wall, and slowly turn down the volume until it disappears. Then I grab the blanket from the end of the couch and drape it around her before silently heading for the door.

"Billy?"

I turn around, and my mother is blinking her eyes open. She seems confused. I move back to her side.

She whispers, "You okay?"

"Yeah, Mom, everything's fine. Go back to sleep."

Her voice grows a little stronger. "Did you have a good time tonight?"

"Yeah, Mom, good times. Go back to sleep."

She starts to sit up more. The blanket falls from her shoulders. She realizes she's wearing the jacket, the hat, she notices the photographs on the table, the glass of wine. She still seems confused, then embarrassed. Her eyes don't hide anything.

"I'm sorry, Billy."

I smile at her. "For what, Mom? Nothing to be sorry about. Don't be sorry."

She starts to cry. I'm surprised by the sudden change. I fall on my knees and give her a hug, but it's my dad's jacket holding me, and the familiar feel and smell of it becomes too much for me. I start to cry too.

My mother sobs, "I'm sorry, I'm so sorry, I'm trying my best."

I answer her, but it's difficult to talk. "I know . . . you are. You're doing great."

Her body's shaking. "I try my best, but sometimes it's just . . . so hard, it really is so hard. I'm not your dad."

"I know you're trying your best. So am I."

She pulls back and looks at me. We're both still crying. "I miss him too, Billy, I miss him so, so much. I'm trying my best."

"I know you are, Mom, I know. I love you."

"I love you too."

We sit at the stop sign. A parade of traffic just keeps zipping by, with no end in sight.

Tess has the Mustang's top down and the heat on; it's a little cold but not too bad. She's playing some music from a mixed CD that I've never heard before. It sounds really good. I bob my head and watch the cars flash by.

Tess keeps inching the car forward. She seems to be getting aggravated.

"I can't believe this traffic!"

I don't know what to say, so I say nothing, just kick back and enjoy the tunes. I watch four crows across the street pecking on a dead squirrel. It almost seems like they're dancing to the music.

"Oh, I'm just going to go for it!"

I look over at her. Her hands are gripping the steering wheel; she's staring down the street. Her skirt is hiked up high on her thigh; I can see her leg muscles twitching in anticipation. What does she mean, "go for it"? There's no break to "go for it." That's all my mother needs, another one of those terrible phone calls.

"Tess, there'll be a break, just wait for it."

"We could be here all day at this rate."

"No, my mom and I always get stuck here. Just when you start to think you'll be here forever, it breaks. You'll see, just wait for it."

She just smiles and punches the pedal to the floor. The car roars forward into traffic, fishtailing and screeching its tires. I close my eyes. The speed of the car pushes me back in my seat. I hear blaring horns behind us but not the expected sounds of crunching metal and breaking glass.

Tess laughs and shouts, "Oh yeah! Tell me that wasn't sweet!"

I open my eyes and look over at her. I'm shocked; I would never have expected her to do something like that. It's like for a moment she was a teenager. She's right, though. Now that I realize we didn't get killed, it was kinda cool.

I can't help but laugh. "That was crazy."

"Crazy fun or just crazy?"

I think for a moment. "Both."

She reaches over and roughs up my hair. "I hate waiting."

We cruise along River Road before heading toward town. Traffic thins out, and Tess lets the car sail down the back streets. The engine roars in satisfaction. Although we're driving well above the speed limit, I'm not scared; Tess seems totally in control. I enjoy watching her drive—there's just something artistic about it. My dad used to love to paint landscapes. He'd have that same look of concentration and satisfaction on his face when he worked.

We slow down by the factory where I had my first driving lesson, and without a word she just whips the car through the entrance and into the back lot.

Tess looks at her watch. "We've got a little time before the poetry reading. I thought maybe another lesson would help you relax a bit."

She's out of the car and walking around toward my side before I've even had a chance to respond. I do better with things like this when I have some time to think about it first. I don't know, maybe I would rather have just gone to the coffee shop and hung out there for a while. I guess she could be right. I am nervous about the reading. Maybe driving will take my mind off of things.

I almost forgot how much fun it is to drive this car. I said "almost." I'm surprised how I'm able to pick up right where I left off. It's a little jumpy for the first minute or two, but then I get right down to it. I drive in huge circles around the parking lot.

Tess tells me she'll teach me how to parallel park next time.

I love the way the setting sun bounces off the hood. I love the feel of these seats, the sound of the engine. I even love the way the car smells.

"Billy, I wanted to ask you something."

I come to a light post and make a large circle around it. "Sure, what's up?"

"Now, don't take this the wrong way, but I've noticed you've been spending a lot of time with Ziggy and Amy."

I smile. "Yeah, I feel like I've got friends again." There's a driveway that goes in a big loop from the parking lot up to the factory and then back again. I point at it with my chin. "Okay if I go there?"

She glances that way. "Sure, no problem. Listen, I have to tell you something. After my father died, I had a really hard time getting my life back to something that resembled normal. It was just so difficult for me, and I spent a whole lot of time by myself and in pain."

I glance over at her. I'm surprised by her sudden confession. I can even see the pain in her eyes. I guess time doesn't really heal everything. Maybe time just helps us get used to things.

"That's how I feel now," I say. "It's . . . hard."

"Believe me, I know. It's a tough place to be. That's why I told you that I'd be here if you needed somebody to talk to, and I really meant that. I wasn't just talking. I want to help. I wish there had been somebody to help me. Understand?"

I slowly turn the car around another light post, keeping my eyes forward. I don't want to look over at her. I'm worried I might start crying; sometimes I don't seem to have any control over that.

"I understand," I say. "Thank you."

"Listen, after my father died, as I said, I spent a lot of time by myself. Then I found a group of kids to do things with. I really thought they were my friends. They made me feel special and I felt like I wasn't so alone anymore. We went to parties and dances—that sort of thing. I felt like I was getting back to being a teenager again. But it took me a really long time to realize that these kids weren't really my friends. They pressured me into drinking and using drugs. I didn't want to lose them as friends, so I just went along with them. I don't want to see that happen to you. I'm worried about your friends."

Where did she get this from? "Ziggy and Amy don't use drugs. I've known Ziggy for years. His dad's a guidance counselor. I know he doesn't use drugs. Amy doesn't use drugs either. There's nothing to worry about."

"I'm sorry, Billy, I'm just trying to look out for you. I'm not saying they use drugs. I just want you to be careful. I don't want you to make the same mistakes I made. Ziggy has that long hair and he's constantly plugged into his iPod—I think you can understand why I'd have reason for concern. Amy seems nice, but you never know. I just want you to be careful, that's all I'm saying."

I slow the car down. Even though Tess seems to mean well, it bothers me that she's questioning my friends. "I understand that you're trying to look out for me, but I don't think you have to worry about Amy or Ziggy."

"How about that other girl I see you with, the one with the long blond hair? She seems a bit wild."

"Julie? She's Ziggy's girlfriend. She's okay."

"Are you sure?"

I stop the car. "Yeah, I'm sure. Shouldn't we be heading over to the coffee shop?"

Tess glances at her watch. "You're right. I guess it's time . . . don't be mad at me, okay? I really am just trying to help. . . . You know what? The coffee shop isn't that far from here. Do you want to drive over there? I think you're ready for some real roads."

I run the idea through my head and find it totally terrifying. "No, I don't really think I'm ready for the main roads yet."

Judging by the near-empty parking lot, Jumping Java's doesn't really seem to be jumping. I guess Friday night isn't a big night for coffee and poetry.

Tess checks her hair in the rearview mirror, then gives me a huge smile. "This is it. Are you excited?"

I'm thinking, *No*, but I answer, "I guess."

"Come on, you're going to knock them all out."

"The parking lot's almost empty. Are you sure there's going to be anyone here to knock out?"

Tess rolls her eyes. "Poets. If there's one thing I can tell you about poets, they're never on time. Don't worry. They'll all be here. Why don't we go in and help set up?"

I grab my notebook from the backseat. It suddenly looks very childish to me. Maybe I should get one of those leather-bound ones. I think I'd look more serious with one of those.

When we start walking toward the front door, it hits me that I'm really nervous. I didn't notice it driving over here, but now it's kicking in big-time. I hope I don't throw up. Now, that would be a great entrance. Walk in the door and shower the room with vomit. Talk about making a lasting first impression.

Tess looks over at me. "Are you nervous?"

"No."

She smiles and opens the door.

There are about seven people in here. I really did expect it to be empty. An old guy with long gray hair pulled back into a ponytail quickly walks over to us. He has a huge smile and an outstretched hand.

105

"Tess, how are you? I haven't seen you in a while. I'm so glad you made it down again."

She reaches out and holds his hand. She doesn't shake it, just holds it. "Jerry, it's so nice to see you. How have you been?"

"Oh, quite well, actually. I went to China over the summer. What an awesome experience."

"China? Business or pleasure?"

"It was business but all pleasure. I sat in for a few weeks as a visiting English instructor. I absolutely loved it. You should think about trying it someday. It's truly rewarding."

"Maybe I will. I'd like to introduce you to a friend of mine. This is Billy Romero. He writes these stunningly beautiful poems. He'll be joining us tonight. Billy, this is Jerry Cook. He teaches English at the community college. This is his group."

Jerry grabs my hand and squeezes it surprisingly hard as he pumps it up and down. "Glad to meet you, Billy. However, I believe that Tess gives me far too much credit. This isn't my group; all I did was hang up a sign. I tend to think of it as *our* group. We're all parts of the whole. All for one and one for all, right?"

"Um, sure."

He smiles. "I hope you have a good time tonight. I'm looking forward to hearing one of your poems. I think you'll find us to be a friendly bunch. I'll introduce you later. Please excuse me. I have to help set up the room."

Tess pats him on the back. "We'll give you a hand. I just want to grab us something to drink."

We walk toward the counter. Suddenly Tess stops and mutters, "Oh, great. That's just great."

"What's the matter?"

She seems really nervous. She looks back at the door and then all around the shop. It looks like she's trying to make up her mind about something.

"Tess, what's wrong?"

She lets out a sigh, points with her chin, and then says in a quick, hushed voice, "See that guy at the counter?"

I look over and see this guy with long hair and a black leather jacket. He's leaning on the counter, flirting with the coffee girl. He looks like he's about sixteen or seventeen, but he somehow seems older.

"Yeah, what about him?"

"I've had some troubles with him in the past. I tutored him a few summers ago. He's obsessed with me. I think there's something wrong with him. He scares me. Can you stick by my side in case I need you?"

"Sure, no problem."

My mother's always telling me how much she needs me, but this is a totally different kind of need. I'm not sure what I'm supposed to do, but I try to stand taller and look tougher.

The guy in the leather jacket turns around. "Tess, I thought that was you. How are you doing? Long time no see and all that."

She answers with no emotion in her voice. It's flat and dry, like sandpaper. "Hello, Drew, how are you?"

"I'm doing great. The band's gonna cut a demo next week. We're all really excited. Hey, I've tried to call you a few times, but the number doesn't seem to work."

"I had it changed, Drew. I told you not to call me anymore."

"Oh, I just wanted to talk, that's all."

"I really don't think we have anything to talk about."

He just stands there for a moment looking at Tess, then he switches his gaze to me. I've never had anyone look at me like this before. It's more of an inspection than a look. I feel like a soldier at boot camp with the staff sergeant staring me down. I stand tall. I act tough. He seems to hate me.

"Who's your little friend?"

Tess inhales deeply, then her voice rises just a little, not enough for anyone around us but Drew to notice. The tone also changes; it now seems sharper, more threatening, like a sentence full of broken glass and nails. "Drew, I think that's enough. I think it's time for you to leave."

The two stand and stare at each other for a moment. Finally Drew snorts, "Yeah, well, I was just leaving anyhow."

He reaches past me to the counter, bumps my shoulder,

and grabs his cup of coffee. Then he gives the cashier a weak smile. "Later, Jenny."

The girl's eyes brighten and her smile grows as wide as it could possibly grow. "Oh yeah, definitely. I work three to six, weekdays. Okay? Good luck next week!"

He takes a few steps past us, then stops and turns around. "Tess, my band still plays at the Lion's Den on Friday nights. I wrote a bunch of new songs. You really should check us out. I think you'd enjoy it."

Tess sighs. "Good-bye, Drew."

His shoulders fall, his face loses what little toughness it once had, and his voice takes on a pleading quality. "Yeah, well . . . you know something? You know what? Why are you like this? I still don't understand it all. I really don't. What did I do?"

"Good-bye, Drew. Do you understand that?"

He shakes his head. "Sure, yeah, I think I understand. I was just hoping I was wrong. . . . Good-bye, Tess."

He gives me a strange look before turning and storming away. As he leaves the shop, he yanks open the door and it slams against the wall. Everybody seems to jump.

Tess lets out a long breath of air, like she's been holding her breath for the last couple of minutes. She lowers her voice. "Thank you so much. He really scares me. I don't know if I could have faced him without you. He gets so violent. Did you see how he crashed that door against the wall? There's something wrong with him. Thanks for your help."

"Um, sure, Tess. But what was that all about?"

"Oh, as I was saying before, I tutored him while I was in college. I needed some extra money. He just got obsessed with me, started stalking me. It was all very strange and scary."

"Did you call the police?"

"The police? Oh, yes, quite a few times. But that's all in the past. Do you want a hot cocoa?"

"What?"

"I said would you like a hot cocoa?"

"I guess . . . so he would, like, follow you around and stuff?"

She opens her pocketbook, looking for her wallet. "Billy, I'd rather not talk about this right now. Okay? I don't want him spoiling our night. We're supposed to be having fun, remember?"

"I guess."

"Stop saying 'I guess.' Try to be decisive. If you can't be decisive, at least try faking it."

"Sorry."

"No need to be sorry, either. The word is meaningless if you hand it out every five minutes like Halloween candy. Hold on." She goes over to the cashier and orders two hot chocolates.

She comes back a moment later and hands me one. "Here you go. Now, I'm sorry; I shouldn't have let him upset me like that. You really have no idea what I've been through. I'm just glad you were there."

"But I didn't do anything."

"You didn't have to—your shining armor was enough. You were there, and I believe that made all the difference. Thank you." She pulls me close and I can smell her perfume; I can feel the softness of her body. She kisses me on the top of the head. I feel like something inside of me just melted away.

She gives me a soft smile. "Why don't we go help Jerry set up?"

The room is surprisingly full. Okay, not full, but there are more people here than I thought there'd be. I counted seventeen. Most of them came in right when we were supposed to start. It's a mix of different ages, mainly late teens and early twenties, but there're a few who are even older. Right now everyone seems more interested in socializing and drinking coffee than reading poetry.

Tess and I sit close together. She's telling me about this horror movie she saw the other night. It sounds pretty cool, but I'm surprised; it doesn't seem like the type of movie she'd like. She asks if there are any movies that I want to see. Before I can answer, Jerry stands up and makes an announcement.

111

"Okay, people, listen up."

Everyone grows quiet and gives him their attention.

"Thank you all for coming down. I want to try to move this along a little quicker tonight. Last week we almost ran out of time. Just a reminder about the regional at the Palace in two weeks. It's going to be very competitive and exciting. I highly recommend that everyone try to attend. Tickets are going real fast. And don't forget, the deadline for the *Poets' Page* contest is just three days away, so you know what that means. Most important, tonight we've got someone new joining us, so let's all give a big welcome to Billy . . ."

He double-checks his notes.

"Romero. Billy, why don't you stand up?"

I can't believe he's asking me to stand up. Tess nudges me in the side, and I slowly rise to my feet. Everybody's looking at me.

"Billy, why don't you say a few words to the group?"

A few words? He wants me to say a few words? Does he think I'm trying to get elected or something? I don't know what to say.

"Um, well . . . I guess, hi, nice to meet you all."

"What's the name of the poem you're going to be reading for us tonight?"

My mouth is dry and I'm starting to get dizzy again. "Um, it's called 'Sour with the Sweet.'"

"Okay, why don't you just jump right in?"

"You want me to go first? I'm not sure I can do that."

"Sure you can. I've found what works best with the newbies is if they just plunge right in and get it behind them."

I just stand there with all of these strange faces watching me. I guess if I ran out the door right now, that would look really lame. "Um, my mind feels like it's all tied up in knots."

Jerry brings out his best wise-old-man smile. "Why don't you give it a try?"

Other voices from the group join his. "Yeah, Billy, give it a try."

"Hey, I want to hear your poem."

"Everyone's nervous the first time, but it's easy, you'll see."

"You'll do great."

Tess says, "It's a great poem. You can do it." Then I feel her slipping the notebook into my hand.

I sigh. "Okay, I'll start first."

The group claps.

I open my notebook and find the poem. Later on I will remember reading the title and then moving into it. I just read it one line to the next line to the next, like walking down a long flight of stairs. It's almost as if someone else is reading it. If I hadn't gone over it a million times with Tess the other night, I'm not sure if I would have been able to do it. I finally get down to my last line; it feels like one of those yellow ribbons stretched out for the winner of a marathon.

When I finish, everyone claps and gives me a little cheer. Jerry tells me that it was "a perfectly structured poem that spoke to me and moved me profoundly." Others in the group say similar things. I feel alive and wonderful. I feel proud and excited. If someone asks me to read another poem, I think I just might do it.

Jerry nods. "That wasn't so bad, now, was it? Good job."

I sit back down in my chair, and Tess puts her arm around me and pulls me close. She whispers in my ear, "Oh, that was just great. I mean it, just great. I'm so proud of you."

I can't help but smile; I can feel it stretching across my face. I also love the feel of her arm around me. I rest my head briefly against her shoulder. A moment later her hand moves up and I can feel her fingers running through my hair, before they slip down and pat me on the back.

She whispers, "I loved it. You have such a great talent."

Jerry looks around the group. "Who wants to go next?"

A girl with long black hair raises her hand. A moment later she's up and reading her poem. I'm still thinking about my reading, and I'm finding it hard to concentrate on hers.

When she finishes, everyone claps and cheers and goes on to tell her what a great poem it was and how it "spoke" to them. It didn't really seem that good to me, but maybe I just wasn't paying attention.

Next one of the old guys reads a poem about his wife's missing cat. This one I manage to listen to, and I think it might be one of the worst poems I've ever heard. I could have written it while sitting on the toilet. Maybe that's how he wrote it; I wouldn't be surprised. When he finishes, I expect stunned silence, but instead the group claps wildly and cheers before going on to praise him.

This goes on for at least another forty-five minutes. One bad poem after another, followed by clapping and praise. I draw portraits of the group to help keep me from losing my mind. I draw Jerry as the evil scientist creating mindless zombies. I'm not sure if the portraits are helping; normally they can get me through anything, but not tonight. I can feel each poem holding my brain hostage. I can feel the desperation and embarrassment of the words; they want to escape these prisons called poems.

Finally Jerry stands up and announces that it's time to take a bathroom break. He puts his fingers in the air and makes air quotes around the word "bathroom." I hate when people do that.

About half the people in the room produce packs of cigarettes and quickly file out the front door.

I turn to Tess and hiss, "This is terrible. I can't take it anymore. Please, can't we leave now?"

"What's the matter?"

"What do you mean, 'what's the matter'? These poems are terrible." I can't help myself, the words just pour out of my mouth. She *must* know I'm right. How could she not?

She leans in close to me. "Not all of them are bad. There are some good poets mixed in the group. They just haven't read yet."

"Can't we just go? Please. How do I know if my poem was any good if they praise every poem? I thought the whole idea of this thing was for me to get an idea of what other people think."

I can tell that Tess isn't happy, but she agrees, and we say our good-byes before heading out to the car.

On the way home Tess surprises me by stopping at this burger place called the Family Room. On Friday nights it becomes a huge high school hangout, and tonight it's packed. At first I feel way out of place with all these older kids around, but after a while I relax. I almost feel like I fit in—almost. I guess tonight's my night for mixing with older crowds.

The burgers and shakes are great. We spend most of the time talking about tonight's poetry club. After a while I get her to admit that the poems we heard were all terrible.

"But yours was really good. I could tell it really blew a lot of people away."

I raise my eyebrows. "How would I know that? They seemed to love everything bad. Maybe if they all hated my poem, I'd feel better about it."

Tess's eyes open wide. "I've got a great idea. The regional! That would be a great place to read your poem. The best poets in the state will be reading there. The winners each get three hundred dollars and their poem published. You would get some excellent feedback and exposure. I think you'd even have a good chance of winning. It's perfect. What do you say?"

"I don't know."

"Say you'll do it. It would be such a great experience for you."

I think about it as I look into Tess's excited eyes. I can tell she really wants me to do this. I guess I've got to learn to take more chances. I didn't think I'd enjoy bowling as much as I did. What if I had decided to stay home that night? Come to think about it, everything good that's happened to me lately has happened because I decided to take a chance. I let the words slip out of my mouth before I spend too much time thinking about what they'll mean.

"Okay, I'll do it."

Tess completely surprises me by squealing, then bouncing out of the booth, running around to my side, and giving me a big hug and a kiss on the cheek. She sits down next to me. "I'm so proud of you! You have such a great talent, it's time you share it."

I look around the restaurant. I notice a table full of guys looking over at me. On their faces I recognize . . . envy.

Dear Dad,

Since you've been gone, every day feels like Halloween. Not the part where you get candy and hang out with your friends. I'm talking about the part where you have to wear a mask. Except that the mask I'm forced to wear looks perfectly normal, at least to those on the outside.

Sometimes I worry the mask will become permanent. That it will just become my new face. Never to be removed. Never to be noticed as just a mask. Never showing what's underneath. Which makes me wonder: How many other people out there are wearing masks? Maybe when you get right down to it, life is just one big meaningless costume ball.

There's so much I don't understand. Bragg keeps telling me that there aren't answers to all of life's questions. He said sometimes you just have to accept things as they are and understand that it's impossible to understand everything. This coming from a guy who's spent the majority of his life studying the basic questions of life. If even he can't come up with a few simple answers, what chance do I have? I told him if I'm stumbling around in the dark, I want someone to tell me where the light switch is, not how to get used to walking around in the dark. He found that very funny. I'm glad I amuse him so much, except I'm not trying to be a comedian. I'm just trying to figure this all out.

The other night I was walking around outside looking at the stars, except it wasn't the stars or the moon that I noticed, it was the darkness that surrounded them. Then I realized that the stars wouldn't be beautiful without the darkness. Is that part of the answer? Or am I just trying too hard?

I have other questions. Questions that aren't as large or complicated. Questions that should have simple answers. Like, what was the last perfect moment we had together? Was it when we went fishing or played catch? Was it when just the two of us went out for lunch, or when we watched that game together? I should be able to pick it out—that should be easy, wouldn't you think? Except that now every moment we ever had together seems like the perfect one, even the times we fought. Even the time you had to go to Europe for three weeks, that was a perfect moment because I knew you'd eventually be coming home.

As much as I hate not being able to pick out a perfect moment, the thought of all the moments we're not going to be able to share together bothers me even more. You'll never meet Amy Wilson, the girl I'm going to my first dance with, or any other girl I'll ever date, or even the girl I'll marry. If one day I have children, you'll never meet them, either. You'll never meet Tess Gate, the English teacher that I do so much with, or any of my other future teachers. You'll never drive me off to college or hear about my first big job. There are so many moments we'll never be able to share together. It rips me apart if I think too much about it. I try not to. I hope you don't mind.

I wish we could just talk. I think that would be enough. I'd love to ask you about Amy. A kid should be able to ask his dad for a little dating advice. Don't you think? But knowing me, I'd be too embarrassed. I'd just stumble off into the dark by myself.

I'd also love to talk to you about Tess, but I'm pretty sure I wouldn't. I don't think I'd be able to because it's all so strange. Sometimes I almost feel like Tess and I are dating. I know that sounds weird, and I don't know why I feel that way. It's just this really messed-up thought that keeps popping into my head. But then I'll think about it and realize that's such an incredibly stupid thing to be thinking. She's so much older than me. I'm just her student. She's just trying to be a friend, and here I am with all these secret thoughts about her. It really makes me feel like a complete idiot. It must be this mask I force myself to wear all day long. It's clouding up my mind. What a dim-witted, moronic, jerky son you have. All this must mean that I've got some kind of schoolboy crush on my English teacher. How pathetic is that?

One day I'm going to rip this stupid mask off and let everyone see what's really underneath. All the tears, all the sadness, all the broken dreams. Hopefully then I'll be able to think clearly. Hopefully then my eyes will be wide open.

I'm standing on the edge of the sidewalk, hands in my jacket pockets, staring into the darkness. My breath puffs out of my mouth in the cool night air. You can tell the cars apart by their headlights. Some are round, some square; some are high, others low. They're all different. A few are almost the same, but they're all different in one way or another.

Amy's mother drives a Volvo. Is that it? Let's see . . . no, headlights are too high. How about that one? No, it's an SUV.

I had my mother drop me off early. I wanted to make sure I got here first. I just didn't like the idea of Amy seeing me drive up with my mother; at least if I got here first, I could be the one waiting for her. I could be the one who opens the door for her. If she's secretly handing out points, that's got to be worth something.

Ziggy told me we should meet him by the pay phone.

He's going to be there with Julie, which sounds great to me—I figure with the four of us we'll always have something to talk about. I told him I was worried about that, and he said that talking is something I definitely shouldn't have to worry about tonight. I wish I had his confidence.

Is that her? Headlights look about right. No, not her, way too small.

I'm shivering. It's cold but not that cold. I must be really nervous. I hope I don't spend the night shaking and stammering. I want to be cool tonight. I don't want anyone to know that this is my first dance or that this is my first real date with Amy.

Is that her? Could be. It's definitely a Volvo. Is it going to turn in? No, it's driving past. Look in the windows, maybe they missed the turn. No, it's an old lady.

I thought about having my mother drive us both to the dance. I paced back and forth in my room thinking about it. I kept running it over and over in my head, and it never seemed to work out. It just seemed like it would be a total disaster.

Oh, this could be her. Let's see, come on, maybe—no, way too big. What was I thinking?

I couldn't imagine my mother driving me to Amy's house. I couldn't imagine the two of us sitting in the backseat together, with my mother up front. All of it would have been way too awkward, and there's no other word for it, awkward.

Hey, this has got to be her. I can tell. All right, stand up tall, shoulders back. Try to look cool, maybe just a little smile. No? I don't believe it. I thought that was her for sure.

Maybe I would have been able to pull off driving with my mom. She can be cool sometimes. Maybe if I had told her beforehand to be quiet and not say anything, that would have worked. I'm just not sure. I wanted to be sure.

In the end my mother and I drove here alone in silence. When we pulled up in front of the school, I said, "I love you," meaning, "May I have twenty bucks?" She kissed me on the cheek and slipped the bill into my hand.

What time is it, anyway? It's kind of getting late. What if she doesn't show up! I didn't think of that before. What would I do? What if she changed her mind?

"Hey, you, what's a girl have to do to get someone to take her to a dance in this town?"

I spin around and she's standing there in her long black coat and felt hat. There's a slight breeze blowing her hair across her face, but I can still see her eyes, her lips, her smile. She looks beautiful.

"Well, sneaking up on the guy always loses a few points."

She walks up to my side and surprises me by hooking her arm through mine and leading me off toward the school. "I didn't sneak up on you. I could have rolled over here on top of a steel drum and I doubt you would have turned around. We also drove right past you. I even waved. Your superhuman powers of observation are scary."

"What? I checked every single car that drove in here. Every single one. I didn't see any Volvos."

"Oh, you were looking for little ole me? I was worried you were looking for a taxi."

My smile grows even larger. "No, I wasn't looking for a taxi. Just you. I'm still not sure how I missed your mom's car."

She sticks her elbow into my side. "You didn't. It's home in our garage. You missed my dad's car."

"Ohhh, the old Trojan horse trick."

"Trojan horse? Hmm, I don't think that works. The Trojan horse was a gift from the Greeks. Now, if a bunch of Greek guys gave you a car and I popped out of the trunk, I think then you could say 'the old Trojan horse trick.'"

"You're pretty smart for a girl."

"Another great line! Now you're oh for two. One more strike and you're outta here."

I hold up my hands and surrender. "Okay, okay. Next pitch I'm sticking my head over the plate and taking one for the team."

She giggles. "The head, huh? I don't know why, but I get the feeling you've taken quite a few for the team."

I open the front door for her. *"Entrez, mademoiselle."*

She tilts her head to the side. *"Merci."*

A thick, slushy wall of sound and cheap cologne almost blasts us both back out the door. I can't believe this is my school. Everything is so incredibly different. Just being here at night is strange enough, but it's more than the time of day. It's everything. Half of the hall lights are turned off. There's a bunch of tables set up against the walls with deep piles of coats on them. There's loud music pouring down the hall. There're signs and banners on the walls, and there are kids everywhere. I mean everywhere; it's beyond crazy, it's beyond Fourth of July in a mason jar, it's just completely beyond anything I expected. Everyone's talking and laughing at the same time. It's a loud, wonderful rat's nest of insanity. I instantly love it.

I feel Amy pushing something into my hand. "What's this?"

"It's your ticket."

"Oh, yeah. What do I owe you?"

She gives me a puzzled look. "I'm taking you. Remember?"

"Well, yeah, but that doesn't mean you have to pay."

"Sure it does. Don't worry about it. Tell you what, if it bothers you, buy me something incredibly expensive someday."

"It's a deal. Just remember, good things come to people who wait."

She raises her eyebrows. "I thought good things come in small packages."

"Um, I think you have to wait twice as long for good things in small packages."

Mrs. Rodriguez, my homeroom teacher last year, collects our tickets. I don't think she recognizes me, which seems strange. You see someone every day for a year, and they forget you in a couple quick months. I hope it's her memory and not me. I don't have to be popular, but I don't want to be forgettable, either.

Amy's pointing down the hall and saying something, but I can't hear her over the noise. I look over in the direction she's pointing and see Ziggy and Julie sitting on the floor by the pay phone.

We head off through the crowd. I reach down and our hands fold together. I'm not sure how it happened. Magnets? Holding her hand is like discovering the power to fly.

Ziggy looks up from the floor. "Dude, you made it. Are you ready to do some dancing?"

I shrug and confess, "I'm not much of a dancer."

He laughs and jerks his thumb toward the end of the hall. "Well, that's okay, because I really don't think what they're doing down there is called dancing. So don't worry about it. Let's just have some fun."

Ziggy lowers his voice and leans close to me. "Oh, just

a heads-up. My dad's chaperoning tonight. He told me he'd stay out of our way, but I wanted you to know so you wouldn't be surprised to see him."

We walk down the hall toward the pounding music. All I can hear is the beat, and it gets louder and softer every time someone opens and closes the door leading into the gym.

When we walk into the gym, I'm amazed by how loud it is. The lights are turned down low, and there's a DJ table set up at the far end of the room. The guy's got four huge speakers pumping out dance music. Ziggy turns to me and yells, "Now do you get blah, blah, blah . . ."

I can't hear him and yell, "What?"

He leans close to my ear and shouts, "Now do you get why I said don't worry about talking?"

I smile and nod.

Amy pulls me close and yells in my ear, "Want to dance?"

I thought that this was going to be my moment of fear. That I would be unable to move, terrified by the prospect of making a complete fool out of myself. In my mind, when I would think about dancing, all I could picture was ballroom dancing. Or I would think of standing in front of Amy and moving my body perfectly to both her movements and the music. But nobody here is doing anything like that. What we have here is a huge blob of kids basically bouncing up and down and shouting. The whole gym has been turned into a large, semicontrolled mosh pit. This doesn't look anything like ballroom dancing; this looks like fun.

I grab her hand and yell, "Let's go!"

The four of us quickly move to the center of the blob and bounce along with the crowd. There's a certain type of rhythm to it. It's like a ceremonial tribal dance with the DJ sitting in for the huge bonfire.

We never grow tired. After about an hour we form a huge circle with a bunch of other kids and start spinning around, holding hands. We keep going faster and faster. I start to get dizzy. Things start flashing before me. The exit doors, the walls, other kids, laughing faces, some teachers against the wall, the basketball hoops, the refreshment table, and then everything suddenly crashes into focus.

There, standing in the corner with her arms crossed, looking straight at me, is Tess Gate.

It really shakes me up at first. I'm not sure why. I guess she's the person I least expected to see right now. I knew that she was a chaperone at the last dance a few weeks ago, and I did bail on our plans for tonight, so I really shouldn't be surprised. Still, it feels strange to see her standing in the corner. She could be floating on a white cloud and I don't think it would feel any stranger.

I try just to focus on my friends. Which isn't too hard. We dance like there's been a twenty-year drought and this is our last chance to make it rain. It's a joyful storm of motion, madness, and laughter.

Throughout the night Tess is never really out of sight or mind. She keeps moving around the outside of the room. She reminds me of a seagull, the way they circle high in the sky, always watchful, always searching, always alone.

Later Ziggy and I are waiting for the girls to come out of the bathroom. Tess walks up to us and asks if we're having a good time. We both agree that it's a great dance. She asks if she can talk to me for a moment.

We walk down to the pay phone. "Billy, I've got a little something for you. I've been meaning to give it to you for a while, but I keep forgetting."

I'm curious. "You've got something for me? What do you mean?"

"I picked you up a present."

"A present? It's not my birthday."

She laughs. "You don't need a birthday to get a present. This is just a little something to show how proud I am of you."

"Proud of me? What did I do?"

"Plenty. You should be proud of yourself too. Remember, I lost my father. I know what you're going through. You're fighting the good fight, and that's something to be proud of. But right now what I'm proud of the most is the way you were able to go out there last Friday and read your poem."

I groan. "Oh, God . . . at the Bad Poetry Society. They would have stood up and cheered the reading of a street sign."

"Maybe so, but that doesn't mean your poem wasn't great. I think, in your heart, you know I'm right. You have more potential than anyone I've ever met before. Listen, come out with me to my car so I can give you your present."

I look down the hall and see Ziggy in front of the

bathroom. He's got his hands buried deep in his pockets and he's staring at the floor. "Outside? Um, I think I should wait for Amy. I don't want her to come out and think I've left her."

"Oh, you've got a lot to learn about girls. Rule number one is it takes us forever to use the bathroom. There are about twenty-five girls in there right now trying to use four stalls. Do the math: We've got time. Besides, I'm parked right out front. It's not going to take us more than a minute."

We walk together into the cool night air. I didn't grab my jacket, and I'm a little surprised at how cold it feels. Tess's car is in the third row. Somehow at night, parked tightly together with the other cars, it just doesn't seem as nice as it has in the past. It almost looks plain.

When we get closer, I notice a big dent in the rear quarter panel. "Tess, what happened to your car?"

"Oh, some moron at the gym just backed right into me. I was shouting and blaring my horn, but he just kept coming."

"Sorry."

"Oh well, that's what insurance is for. Right?"

"I guess."

She unlocks her door and then leans into the backseat to get my present. Her skirt rises up high as she fishes through a bag. It seems to be taking her a long time to find it. Judging from the look of Tess's legs, she must spend a whole lot of time at that gym. My eyes feel drawn to them, but I quickly feel guilty as her skirt keeps rising higher.

I look away. I gaze up into the night sky. The stars are spread out across a clear, endless field of darkness. I suddenly feel very small, swallowed by the vastness of it all.

A shooting star flashes across the sky. I make a wish. I have to think about it for a minute but settle on: *Happiness for my family.*

I feel Tess by my side. "It's beautiful, isn't it? It's the end of our earthly boundaries, but at the same time the beginning of endless possibilities."

"I guess."

She points. "Look, can you see Orion?"

I look, but I can never seem to find constellations. "No, not really."

"Oh, it's so clear." She comes behind me and puts her arms over my shoulders. She puts her left hand under my chin and gently moves my head up and a little to the side, and then points over my right shoulder with her other arm.

She speaks in a hushed tone into my ear. "Here, follow my arm. Do you see it now? Orion is the hunter. Can you see his sword? And there's his body, the three stars form his belt, see it?"

I can see it. "Oh, yeah, now I do. That's cool."

I can feel Tess's body up against my back; I'm aware of

every single inch that touches me. My knees feel weak. I find it difficult to breathe, to swallow, to stand.

She points a little to the side. "There're his two dogs, Canis Major and Canis Minor. Orion was a great hunter. He hunted Taurus the bull." She moves her arm and my head in its direction. I surrender to her guiding hands like a puppet. "And Lepus the rabbit." She shows me Lepus.

I can smell her perfume, her hair, the sweetness of her breath.

"Orion was madly in love with Merope, one of the seven sisters. His desire for her burned so strongly he worried it would consume him in fire. She's over here in the Pleiades star cluster." Her finger traces a circular pattern in the sky. "I have a hard time finding her, but she's one of those bright stars. Merope didn't feel anything for Orion and wouldn't return his affections. One day Orion accidentally stepped on Scorpius, the scorpion, and died.

"The gods felt sorry for him," she continues, "for one who loved so strongly and completely, yet never had his affections returned. They blessed him by turning him into a constellation. They gave him his dogs, along with Taurus and Lepus to hunt."

Tess moves her arm across the sky, indicating something that can't be seen. "And to keep Orion safe, they placed Scorpius so the two would never again occupy the same sky."

We stand quietly together, gazing up at the sky. Tess rests her hands on my shoulders. I want to say something to fill the silence but can't think of anything. Time starts to stretch on, moving at a completely new and different pace. I feel comforted by her hands on my shoulders and the closeness of her body. For some reason I close my eyes and slowly sink into the moment.

Her hand moves up and gently caresses my cheek. I shiver with both surprise and excitement. I open my eyes and quickly move away.

Tess seems startled by my sudden movement and quickly grabs something off the roof of her car. She fumbles with it and stammers, "Oh, here's your . . . present. I hope you . . . I hope you like it."

She hands me a package about the size of a shoe box. It feels light but far from empty. I smile, but even I'm not sure if it's a real smile or a forced one. "Um . . . thank you."

"You're welcome, but do me a favor, don't open it now. Open it later. When you get home. Okay?"

"Why?"

"Oh, it's just the way I've always been. I know it's strange. If someone opens a present and I can tell they don't like it, I feel bad. If they open it and really like it, I feel embarrassed. It's easier for everyone if they just open it by themselves."

"Okay. If that's what you want."

I stand there awkwardly for a moment, holding the

present by my side. I almost feel like I should give her a kiss, but I can't get myself to do it. I take a step forward but stop. Finally I say, "Well, okay . . . I really should be getting back to my friends."

"Okay . . . sure, I guess you should."

I turn and jog to the school, holding the present like a football. I bound up the stairs and through the front door.

I look down the hall and see Ziggy waiting with the girls and quickly run down to join them.

"Dude, what took you so long?"

Everyone's looking at me. "Sorry. Miss Gate just wanted to give me this present."

"What did you do? Go to the store together, pick it out, and have them wrap it?"

I can feel my face getting red. "No, we just kinda talked for a while. That's all."

Amy walks to my side and looks at the box. "Well, open it up."

"Oh, she wants me to wait until I get home to open it."

She gives me a strange look. "That's odd, don't you think? The whole thing's kind of odd. Why did she give you a present, and why tonight? You see her every day at school. It's kind of bizarre to give it to you now."

"She said she keeps forgetting to give it to me. I guess it's for doing well at the poetry reading."

Amy rolls her eyes. "And what are you supposed to do with it now? Just carry it around for the rest of the night?"

I admit I didn't think about that. Luckily Ziggy's dad is one of the chaperones. Zig talks to him for a moment, gets his car keys, takes the box from me, and runs it out to his car. I'm driving home with them anyhow, so it works out fine. Problem solved.

The rest of the evening flies by. I don't really see Tess much after that. She's there but seems to be spending most of the time talking to some teachers in the far corner. Before I know it, they're flashing the lights telling everyone it's time to go home.

It takes us a while to find our coats; somehow they all got thrown off the table, and they're in a big heap on the floor. The whole time we're looking for them, I keep thinking about the best way to say good night to Amy. Should I hug her and give her a kiss? Should I just hug her instead? Would she let me kiss her? Should I kiss her on the lips or on the cheek?

When we leave the school, we practically run right into Amy's dad. She introduces me and we shake hands. He seems like a nice guy.

Amy turns to me. "Well . . . bye. I had a really good time."

"Yeah, me too. It was great."

greg logsted

This isn't the good-bye I've been fantasizing about. It's funny how little control we have over the future.

Amy surprises me by quickly moving in close, going up on tiptoes, and kissing me on the cheek.

I must look as stunned as I feel, because even Amy's dad smiles.

138

I saw this movie. I forget the name of it. There's this scene toward the beginning of the film: It's in a crowded restaurant. There are all these people just living their lives. Some are having lunch, others a drink. Everybody's talking and laughing. A man kisses his girlfriend. Two college guys are arguing about a soccer match. A table in the corner is singing "Happy Birthday." A group of businessmen are signing documents. Waiters and waitresses are working hard.

It's just a normal day in a restaurant, a day like any other day.

A man gets up and starts to walk toward the front door. This little girl notices a wrapped present the man has forgotten under his table.

The girl says, "Daddy, look. That man forgot his present."

The father sees it and quickly stands up and calls out

to the man, "Excuse me, sir. Excuse me. You forgot your present!"

The man pretends not to hear him and walks faster.

The father calls out to him again, but he still doesn't turn around; instead the man panics and starts to run, knocking over a tray of dishes on his way out the door.

There's a moment of silence. The camera quickly moves from face to face in the restaurant; you can see the fear and confusion in their eyes. They know there's something in that wrapped box. They sense something terrible is about to happen.

The camera moves outside. It's a peaceful, quiet, sunny day. A moment later there's the roar of a loud, powerful explosion. The windows and doors of the restaurant are blown out, and debris showers across the sidewalk and street.

For some reason I keep thinking of that movie whenever I look at this present that Tess gave me. I haven't opened it yet. It's just sitting on my kitchen table. Just sitting there like a big orange in a bowl of apples. I can't even get myself to touch it. I keep looking at it. Walking around it. Wondering about it. Worrying about it. The wrapping paper has these little clowns on it; they all seem to be laughing at me, mocking me, daring me to unwrap the box.

I should open it. What's the big deal? Just open it and be done with it. I know it's not a bomb or anything like that. I just have this real bad feeling about it.

I can't sleep. It's not like when my father died and I couldn't sleep. This is completely different. Then it was this suffocating sadness that kept pressing down on my chest; tonight it's a type of excitement, a big ball of energy, like I swallowed the sun. It pulls me to my feet and makes me walk around the house. It makes me rewind and play the evening over and over again in my head.

The dance now feels more like a movie than a memory. Somehow by rewinding and playing it more times than I can count, it has become less real, less solid, less like something that actually happened to me. I've become just an actor playing and replaying the same few scenes in my life until they become almost meaningless. I guess if you look at anything too closely, it starts to lose its wonder. It's like a painting: You have to stand back and look at the whole thing to see its beauty; if you get up close and look at each and every brushstroke, it becomes nothing more than just paint on canvas.

"You still up?" My mother interrupts my thoughts by walking into the kitchen.

"Yeah, can't sleep."

She sits down beside me. "You had a good night tonight, huh?"

"Yeah, it was great."

"Amy sounds like a really nice girl."

"Yeah, she is. I really like her."

"I can tell."

She points her chin at the present. "Are you ever going to open that gift from your teacher?"

"I guess."

"What's the problem?"

"I don't know, Mom. I just get a bad feeling about it. I don't know why. Maybe I shouldn't open it. Maybe I should just give it back to her."

She picks up the present and shakes it. "I thought the whole thing was kind of strange. Walking in here from a dance with a gift from your teacher. Now you've got me really curious. I want you to open it."

"I dunno."

"Billy, open the present."

I unwrap it. Inside there's a shoe box. "Nike? She got me sneakers? That's weird."

My mother picks up the box. "No, it's too light for sneakers. Open the lid."

I pull off the top. Inside there's something wrapped in paper. I take it out and unwrap it. There are two books of poetry by Pablo Neruda, *Residence on Earth* and *Twenty Love Poems and a Song of Despair*.

My mother thumbs through the books. "Hmm, Pablo Neruda. I studied him in college. He's a great poet, maybe a little too adult for you, but he certainly is a great poet."

I find a card at the bottom of the box and take it out. My mother leans over my shoulder. We read it together.

Dear Billy,

I just wanted to give you a little something to show you how proud I am of you. You did a fantastic job with your poem. Your poems touch me in much the same way as Pablo Neruda's do. You are extremely talented, so please don't be discouraged.

Here are two volumes of Neruda's poems. I think you will really enjoy them, especially TWENTY LOVE POEMS AND A SONG OF DESPAIR.

You're a very special person. I feel blessed to have met you.

Love,

Tess

My mother picks up the note and reads it a second time. "Hmm, maybe it's time for 'Tess' and me to have ourselves a little talk."

"You gonna eat your pudding?"

I look across the table at Chris Dalton. His chubby face, his sunken eyes, his hair that looks like it hasn't been combed in a year.

"Nah, you can have it." I slide it across the table and he attacks it. It's been about two weeks since Mr. Knight told me I should try to be nicer to Chris, and I've been trying, but the guy doesn't make it easy. All he seems to want to do is eat.

The thing is, about two years and forty pounds ago Chris sat next to me in my sixth-grade class. We were friends. I used to enjoy hanging with him. I don't know what happened. He just changed. He doesn't joke around anymore or laugh, doesn't really even talk to anyone. He just shuffles around all day looking at his feet. I know everyone changes a lot between sixth and eighth grades, but Chris turned into a completely different person.

"Hey, Chris?"

He looks up from the dessert. "Yeah?"

"Um, how was the pudding?"

He gives me a suspicious look. "Fine . . . why?"

"No reason, just asking."

"You didn't put anything in it, did you?"

I quickly shake my head. "No, no really, I didn't."

"You didn't spit in it or anything?"

"No! Why would I do that?"

"I dunno. Just askin'. . . . Somebody did that to me last week."

I hold up my hands. "I'm sorry. You've got to know that I would never do anything like that."

He stares at me for a couple of seconds, then huffs, "Yeah, I know. Sorry."

"Actually, I want to ask you something."

He gives me another suspicious look. "What?"

"Are you . . . are you okay?"

He snorts. "I'm fine, just like to eat, that's all."

"No, I mean . . . well, I mean . . . how's life?"

He shakes his head and just looks at the table for the longest time. Finally he looks up and says in a bitter tone, "You really want to know? It . . . it stinks."

I don't know what to say but realize I've got to say something. "Um, why? What's wrong?"

He looks down and starts moving stuff around on his plate with his fork. "Cancer."

"Oh, God! You've got cancer?"

He shakes his head but still avoids looking at me. "No. Not me, my mom does. It's my mom."

"She gonna be okay?"

He doesn't say anything for a real long time. Finally he sighs and says, "You know, I don't think so. She got sick two years ago, and she just seems to be getting sicker."

"I'm sorry, Chris. I didn't know. I think maybe you should have said something or . . ." I can't seem to find the right words.

"What's there to say? All I want to do is get through my days at school."

I look hard at this eighth-grade version of Chris: He's puffy, depressed, and slow moving, but I can still see my old sixth-grade friend buried inside him. He must be going through the same kind of stuff I've been going through. Why didn't I notice that before?

"I'm sorry, I didn't know. We used to be tight—you could've talked to me."

He looks at me. "I wanted to. I wanted to talk to somebody, but I just couldn't. It's like I just have enough inside me to struggle through the days. I'm not like you."

"Like me? What do you mean, like me? What are you talking about?"

He looks back down at his tray. "After your father died. I couldn't believe how quickly you came back to school.

How you were able to go to your classes again. How you talked to your friends. I even heard you laugh. I want to be like you."

I can't believe what I'm hearing. "You want to be like me? I've been a complete mess. You don't want to be like me. Why not pick one of the kids at the popular table over there? Look at them—good looking, good at sports, have the girls hanging around them. Why not be like one of them?"

"They might be popular, but that doesn't make them strong."

My voice grows louder in frustration. "I'm not strong. It's tough for me to make it through the day. Sometimes I worry I'm just going to start crying in the middle of class."

Chris leans forward and points his finger. "But you don't . . . that's the thing, you don't . . . you control yourself . . . and you have your drawings and your poetry. That's why I started sitting with you at lunch. I wanted to see what you were doing, what you were drawing, what you were writing. I wanted to try to be strong like you. I was even hoping some of it would rub off on me."

I don't know what to say. I just sit there like a broken hourglass with my sand slowly spilling all over the floor. "I'm not the person you think I am. I'm not. Sometimes I go through whole days in a thick fog. I even have to go see a shrink every week."

"So do I."

"Really? I thought I was the only kid in school seeing a shrink. Who do you see?"

He runs a hand through his thick hair. It's like watching someone try to rake leaves with a fork. "A guy here in town. His name's Dr. Bragg."

A laugh escapes from my mouth. "Dr. Christopher W. Bragg?"

"Yeah."

"That's who I see! No wonder you're not getting any better." I keep laughing. I can't help myself.

I put my hand on my chin like Bragg always does and imitate his slow, plodding voice. "So . . . tell me, Chris, how does it feel to be . . . nuts, to be . . . bonkers, to be . . . out of your mind?"

I notice that Chris is smiling. Not just a little smile, but a big, wide one. It's the first smile I've seen on his face since the sixth grade.

I get up and walk around the table. I sit next to him. I don't know if the other kids are looking at us right now, and I really don't care. In a hushed voice I say, "Listen, Chris, we're buds. I'm here for you, okay?"

"If I was having dreams about dancing turtles, what would that mean?"

Dr. Bragg leans forward with his hand on his chin. "Are you having dreams of dancing turtles?"

"No."

"Then, why are you interested in dancing turtles?"

"I'm not."

He leans back in his leather chair and it makes a farting sound. Normally stuff like that doesn't crack me up, but for some reason today it really seems funny. Luckily I manage to control myself and I don't laugh.

"Billy, why are we talking about dancing turtles?"

I look past his shoulder. There's a window behind him, and you can see the street entrance of the office complex through it. I'm looking for Tess's red Mustang; she's going to be meeting my mother at the coffee shop downstairs.

"I guess I was just wondering about dreams."

"Are you having bad or strange dreams?"

"No."

"Then, what is it about dreams that causes you to raise this question?"

I lean back in my chair. "I guess I'm just curious about dreams. What do they mean? That's all."

"Personally, I don't put a whole lot of stock in trying to analyze dreams. Sometimes they can be meaningful, but just as likely they're totally meaningless. If you had a dream about dancing turtles, I'd say it's probably just your imagination having a little fun and relaxation. If you're having dreams about dancing turtles every night, I'd say maybe it's time we sit down and figure out what's going on."

"Hmm, interesting."

Bragg leans forward in his chair; it makes the farting sound again. "Billy, what's going on? You seem terribly distracted today."

I'm looking out the window. I can see Tess's car waiting at the light; she has the top down and her turn signal on. It seems too cold to be driving around with the top down. I bet she has the heat blasting. I bet she's got the music blasting too.

"Billy?"

"Huh?"

"Are you okay?

"Sure, why?"

His left eyebrow rises up the way it does when he's getting aggravated. "Well, because I'm talking and you're not listening to a word I'm saying."

"Sorry. Maybe I am just a little . . . distracted or something." I can see Tess turning into the complex. She's wearing sunglasses. Her hair is flowing in the breeze.

"Can you tell me what's distracting you?"

She's driving toward the building. She's almost at the point where I'm not going to be able to see her anymore. There: She moves out of my sight, beneath the windowsill.

"What?"

"Like my old high school football coach used to say, 'You gotta keep your head in the ball.'"

She must be pulling in front of the coffee shop now. Finding a spot. Parking her car.

I focus on Bragg. "What? . . . No . . . what are you talking about?"

"I'm talking about you. Why can't you seem to focus today?"

I bet she's out of her car right now, heading for the front door. My mother's probably looking up from her coffee. Maybe they've made eye contact. Tess seems like the type to always wave first. I wonder if she'll open the front door herself, or will some guy rush to open it for her?

"I'm sorry, Dr. Bragg. I guess I'm just tired. Can I ask you something?"

"Does it involve dancing turtles?"

"What? . . . No, no dancing turtles."

He moves around in his chair. I wait for the farting sound, but it doesn't happen this time. "Ask away, but I think it's only fair that I get the next question."

"Is Chris Dalton a patient of yours?"

Bragg makes a clucking sound with his tongue. "I'm sorry. I can't reveal who is or who isn't one of my patients. It's not ethical."

"But he told me he was your patient."

"Be that as it may. I cannot discuss the specifics of any other present or potential client. I hope you understand. Privacy is an important element of both my practice and my patients' treatments."

"But he's a friend of mine. I want to help him."

"Billy, I'm sorry. I can't. Do you have any other questions?"

I think about it for a moment and get an idea. "Yeah, um, I've got this other friend, his name is, um . . . Jack. His mother is dying, and he's having a real hard time coping with it. He's depressed and withdrawn. I want to help him. Could you give me some advice?"

Dr. Bragg smirks and shakes his head before standing up. He paces around the room in silence for a minute. Finally he says, "Now, it's difficult for me to comment on someone who I've never had time to sit down with. So whatever advice I can offer you will have to be general as opposed to specific. I hope that's agreeable."

I nod.

"It sounds as if your friend Jack is going through something called anticipatory grief. It's important to realize that the best thing you can do for your friend right now is to just be there for him. Remember, humans are social creatures, and we all need interpersonal feedback. Tell you what. Let me get a pen and paper and a good booklet or two on the subject. We'll go over a couple of things together that I think will be helpful. Hold on, I'll be right back."

I wonder how my mom and Tess are doing. Are they talking quietly together, maybe even whispering, or are they fighting loudly? Are they comfortable with each other or very uncomfortable? I really don't think I did anything wrong. Maybe I did and didn't realize it; I guess that's possible. Sometimes I feel like I'm standing on top of an avalanche with everything quickly sliding out from underneath me.

The elevator doors slide open and I'm surprised to see my mom standing there. I try to read her face, but it's blank. I quickly scan the room, looking for Tess, but she's nowhere in sight.

"How did it go, Mom?"

"Fine, hon. We'll talk in the car, okay?"

I follow her out to the car. I'm trying to read her mood, but I just can't get a feel for it. It's almost like she's happy and sad at the same time.

We drive in a cold, solid silence for at least a half mile. My mother has her hands placed firmly on the steering wheel, her eyes focused forward. I do my best to remain perfectly still, desperately trying to keep the discomfort from seeping out of my skin and filling the car. I can't take this silence much longer; it's getting way too thick. If I had a knife, I'd slice it into little bite-size pieces and start dropping them out the window.

My mother clears her throat and says, "Billy, you should have told me what was going on."

Wham! What does she mean by that? What am I supposed to say? I decide to use the multipurpose, never-fails answer.

"What do you mean?"

"If you had told me, it wouldn't have been such a complete shock. I could have asked different questions. Maybe I could have avoided all of Tess's tears."

"Miss Gate cried?"

"Yes, it was completely unexpected."

"What did she cry about?"

My mother seems to be losing her patience. "What do you think she cried about?"

"I don't know. I wasn't there."

154

"Her father. Why didn't you tell me her father died when she was your age?"

"I don't know. Just didn't, I guess."

"It put me in a very awkward spot. I felt so sorry for the girl. It's obvious what's going on here. She's trying to make up for the loss of her own father by trying to help you deal with the loss of yours. It's actually very sweet. I think she might just be trying too hard."

"I guess."

I look out the window and watch some little kid trying to walk a huge dog. It's pulling him down the sidewalk like an ox pulls a plow.

She smiles. "Actually, Tess is quite special in her own way. After she calmed down, we got a chance to talk. I mean really talk, and I must admit I was very impressed. She's had a tough life, but she never gave up. She's a real fighter. Did you know that she put herself through college? She's also done extremely well buying and selling rare books online. I had no idea you could make so much money doing something like that."

We drive over the Clinton Street bridge. The car always makes a weird thumping sound here, so my mother stops talking for a second.

"She's also been thinking about doing some investing in real estate. It might be perfect for her; I believe she has just the right mix of personality and intelligence to be very successful at it. Actually, we might get together next week and look over a few things together.

"Oh, I'm also going to try to join you guys for the regional poetry competition this Saturday, but like I was telling Tess, it might be tough for me to get away from work."

It starts to rain, a hard, driving rain. My mother switches on the wipers, then turns them up to the highest speed. They slap back and forth like frantic little men desperately trying to bail out a sinking ship with coffee cups. I didn't notice the gathering storm clouds. I guess it happened while I was with Dr. Bragg.

I remember that we have a huge umbrella in the hall closet that we never use. It just stands in the corner. It's always falling down when you try to hang up a coat.

"Mom?"

"Yeah."

"Remember that big umbrella we bought you for your birthday?"

"What about it?"

"We should keep it in the trunk of your car."

I look up from my poem and see a pebble that's a little smaller than a marble. It just flew off the back of a yellow pickup truck. I'm not sure how I can even see something that small from this far away. I know it's going to hit our windshield. I don't know why I know that. I just do. I feel like I'm some kind of road-hazard magnet pulling it toward us. It's moving down the highway like a Slinky. Moving from one lane to the other with a strangely determined, bouncy march. It's getting closer. Here it comes. It's in the other lane. It takes one last suicidal bounce toward us.

Smack! It's louder than I would have thought. A spiderweb-like crack instantly appears and runs across the whole windshield.

Tess slams her hand on her steering wheel and shouts, "Oh, man! I don't believe it!"

I sit perfectly still. I don't say a word. I learned a long

time ago to stay away from rage; it's very sticky. Touch it wrong and you get it all over yourself.

Tess turns and shouts, "Did you see that?"

I don't know what to say. What does she want me to say? Of course I saw it. It hit the windshield—how could I not see it? I decide just to go with the standard, "I'm sorry."

She snaps, "You're sorry. What do you have to be sorry about? Stop saying you're sorry about everything. It's getting really, really annoying."

Sticky rage. I knew better, but I just had to touch it.

Tess pounds on the steering wheel again. "First my rear quarter panel, now the windshield. My car's starting to look like crap!"

I turn my attention back to my notebook and start going over my poem. Maybe if I just ignore her, she'll calm down. I'm slowly reading each line, but I just can't seem to concentrate. Why did Tess yell at me? What did I do? I feel the anger building up in me to the point where I can barely even think straight.

I give up trying to study my poem and just stare out my window and watch the other drivers. They all seem to be in some kind of a trance; maybe they're making mental lists of things to do when they get home or things to buy at the mall. I wonder how many of them worry about accidents. It takes only a second to lose someone you love. I never used to think like that, but now everything seems so fragile, like constantly walking on thin ice. We pass the man in the yellow pickup. He's singing along to his radio. It looks like he's really belting out a tune; he seems very happy. I wonder if my dad was singing.

I feel Tess's hand on my shoulder. "I'm sorry, Billy. I was just upset about my windshield. I didn't mean to snap at you."

"Whatever."

"Come on, don't be like that. I said I was sorry."

I give her an icy, "Fine."

We drive in silence. I can feel my anger slithering into the car like a poisonous snake. I'm sure by now its presence must be known.

I hear sniffling and look over at Tess. I see tears running from under her sunglasses and down her cheeks.

"You're crying?"

She wipes her cheek with the sleeve of her sweater. "I'm just upset about my car. I didn't mean to yell at you."

"Why are you crying?"

"Because I'm spoiling the day. You should be focused on the regional. You should be practicing your poem. I'm spoiling everything."

"Don't cry anymore, okay? This isn't worth crying about. Save your tears for bigger things. Everything's fine."

She looks over the top of her sunglasses. "Really?"

"Yes, really."

She gives me a weak smile, wipes away a remaining tear, then reaches around my shoulder, pulls me close, and kisses me on the forehead. "Let's start over and have ourselves a good time, okay?"

"Okay."

It's funny how I can be so mad at someone one moment and then just let it go the next. I guess tears melt away my anger. I had no idea they could be that powerful.

"Oh, guess what? I know your mom had to work today, but I brought my camera. I'll make her some video so she can watch you later."

"Thanks. She'd like that."

"I was really hoping she'd be able to join us today."

"Yeah, me too, but Saturday's a tough day for her to take off."

She suddenly reaches into the back and starts looking through a gym bag. "You've got to hear this new mix CD. It's great. You're going to love it . . . if I can find it. I know it's here someplace."

"Tess, I think that's our exit."

She snaps forward and starts spinning the wheel and pumping the brake. Horns are blaring all around us. "Hold on! I think we can make it!"

I reach out and hold on to the dashboard. I'm not sure we can.

● ● ●

We drive past the front of the old Palace Theater. It's one of those theaters that have been around forever but now only show older movies. I used to come here a lot with my dad; it was worth the drive because they charge only about three bucks to get in. They also make fantastic popcorn with real butter.

There's a huge banner hanging out front with bold red letters announcing, THE FIFTH ANNUAL REGIONAL POETRY COMPETITION. Below the sign there's a line of people waiting to get in.

I never expected this many people. The parking lot is packed. Everyone seems to be in their late teens or early twenties, but I also see a lot of older people too.

Tess's car roars our arrival as we drive up and down the lanes searching for an open spot. I think we're driving a little too fast but don't say anything.

We manage to find a parking spot before running over any small children or old ladies.

"Name, please."

I just stand there. I can't believe all these people. There must be thirty people back here and at least three hundred out front in the theater. I never expected it to be like this. I feel like I've been sleeping and just woke up in a completely different world.

"What's your name?"

Everyone's pacing around, talking to themselves, practicing their poems. Some are doing loud voice exercises, while others rehearse facial and body movements in front of a large mirror. There's a thick current of tension buzzing throughout the room.

"I need your name."

Tess leans forward. "His name is Billy Romero."

This bushy-haired guy with thick black plastic glasses starts checking names on a clipboard. "Let's see, Romero, Romero, hmm, let's see."

He looks up. "Sorry. I don't see a Romero."

Tess snaps, "That's impossible! We sent in a check last week, and I called yesterday for confirmation."

"Oh, why didn't you say so? If you sent it in last week, he'll be on the late-entrants list." He turns over a few pages on the clipboard. "Let's see . . . yeah, here it is. You're going to be number seven. Lucky seven."

He hands me a piece of paper with a seven on it. The number looks bigger and bolder than I feel.

I mumble, "Thanks," and just stand there. I feel like this small piece of paper just tied me down in the path of a train.

Tess grabs my elbow and gently pulls me into the back room; the walls seem to grow darker. Once we're inside, it becomes even more chaotic. Everyone seems nervous and excited. I stand in the middle of the room, while the other contestants move quickly around me practicing their lines. I feel like I'm standing in the eye of some strange energy storm. It sure is different from the Bad Poetry Society at Jumping Java's.

These poets all seem to be possessed by creative powers far greater than mine. Mountains of talent surround me, and I feel lost and overshadowed in my little ordinary valley below.

Tess is still holding on to my elbow. It reminds me of when I first learned to ride a bike without training wheels. My dad took them off and ran by my side, holding on to my elbow. Just like Tess is doing now. We went up and down the street a few times together.

After a while he shouted, "I'm letting go!" I went on alone. My front tire wobbled at first, but I didn't crash. It was more exciting than I would ever have imagined. I started to laugh. I felt free and proud. I grew more confident and pushed myself to go faster, but then I turned my wheel a little too quickly and started to go down. The hard asphalt road came rushing up toward me. I put out my hands to break the fall, fully expecting a painful landing. My dad swept me up in his arms just before I hit the ground; he'd been running behind me the whole time, but I hadn't realized it.

"Are you okay?" Tess is looking at me strangely, expecting an answer. I keep thinking about that hard asphalt road rushing toward me.

"This is really going to hurt, isn't it?"

She takes me over to this large, empty coat closet and closes the door behind us. There's a chair in the far corner. "Here, sit down. I think it's time for you to take a few quiet moments and relax. Don't worry or think about what others are doing; just focus on yourself. You are going to do great. You're getting yourself all worked up for nothing."

I can feel my heart beating faster; it's actually getting harder to breathe. I hope I don't throw up. I reach up and wipe my forehead; my hand comes back covered with sweat. It shines under the fluorescent light, a handful of fear.

Someone in the outer room bellows, "Contestant number one starts in two minutes. You're all welcome to watch from the wings, but do not disturb the performers. Good luck to all, and to all, good luck!"

"Tess, I don't think I can do this."

She kneels down beside me. "Yes, you can. I know you can."

"Everyone is so much older and better than me. What am I doing here?"

She grabs my hand. "They may be older, but they're not any better. You're a great poet."

I look into her blue eyes. I can feel tears starting to flow down my cheeks. Why am I crying? I can't believe this is happening to me.

I moan, "I can't do this. I'm too scared. I just can't. Really."

She puts her arms around me and pulls me close. I can feel her body, her hair, the softness of her cheek against the side of my head. Everything becomes this moment, like that second right after the sun sets and night overtakes the day.

She kisses me on the top of the head. "Oh, my sweetness. Please don't cry. It's going to be okay."

For some reason, her mentioning my tears makes me cry even harder. It becomes difficult to talk. "I don't know . . . if I can do this. I just . . . I just don't know."

She kisses me on the forehead. "Don't you cry. I can't stand to watch you cry."

"No, you don't understand. It's too much, everything's become too much . . . I'm too full . . . I'm going to burst like a balloon."

She kisses me on the cheek. "It's okay, everything's going to be okay."

She kisses me again on the cheek, the temple, the neck. She stops for a moment, and I can feel something inside of me sliding away.

I close my eyes and surrender to it. I fall into this new soft and tender darkness.

I suddenly feel Tess's lips on mine. Everything in the world stops and spirals outward, rushing to a point beyond silence.

Without thinking, I move forward and kiss her back. We kiss a third time. It's like a strong undertow has grabbed me and I'm being pulled out to sea.

I want to kiss her again and again, but she moves away.

Tess rests her forehead against mine. I open my eyes and see tears running down her cheeks. She looks into my eyes and whispers, "I'm sorry, I couldn't help myself."

Tess and I are sitting together on the floor, off to the side of the stage. She's holding my hand. Her leg is pressed up against mine. Contestant number five is bouncing around behind the podium. He's fantastic. I have no illusions that my poem is better than his. It's not. As a matter of fact, I'll be surprised if my poem is better than anyone's today. All of these people are just in a class far above me. I can learn a lot if I open my eyes and pay attention.

The moments Tess and I shared together in the closet were unlike anything I'd ever experienced before. The world outside melted away. I'll always remember those three kisses. She held me close for a long time, while whispering words of encouragement; it made me feel important, proud, and handsome. After a while I started to calm down.

I'm still finding it hard to believe that she kissed me. Did I do something wrong? Is that why my fantasies are becoming realities? I didn't think things like this happened in real life. Does this mean that she loves me or likes me, or does it mean nothing at all? Was she just trying to calm me down, or did she really want to do that? Will she kiss me again, or will that be the only time?

I know I'm not going to win today. I know I'm not going to find answers to all my questions, but facing and conquering my fears, now that's a huge goal. That's something I can reach out and hold on to. Something that's definitely real. Something I understand. That's the target that hangs on the wall. If there's one thing that Tess convinced me of today, it's that there are no losers here. There's just first, second, and third; everyone else comes in fourth.

Who knows? Maybe a few people out there will listen to the words I wrote alone in my bedroom and find them entertaining. That's all I'm really hoping for now. Tess told me that I should form my own ten percent club. If only ten percent of this crowd likes my poem, I should call it a good day.

Tess is right: I can do this.

Contestant number six is on the stage. She's a short girl with long black hair and a bright red shirt. I'd say she's around twenty, maybe a little older. I guess that means I'm next. Time seems to be moving at a strangely different pace.

She's amazing. It's a hip-hop-style poem. The crowd is so into her. She's bouncing and moving her hands to the words. She's pointing and shouting. I can't believe how wonderful she is. I can't believe I have to go out there next.

It's going to be like comparing a candle with the sun.

I look at my poem, but I can hardly read it because my hands are shaking so much. My legs start to shake. I'm getting dizzy again. I feel like I'm about to get sick.

"Tess, I can't do this." The words burst out of my mouth. Something flickers in her eye. Disappointment? I can tell she thought I had conquered my fear.

"We went over this. You can do it. Remember the ten percent club."

I look at Tess. She seems so determined that I get out there. I don't want to let her down and I'd like to make her proud, but I'm just not sure I'm capable of doing this. I'm not sure I'd even be able to read a grocery list right now.

"I think I'd pass out."

She puts her arm around me and pulls me close. "I know you can do it."

"No, Tess, I really can't."

"Billy Romero." An amplified voice is calling my name. I look out at the stage, and the bushy-haired guy is looking at me. It can't be my time already. What happened to number six? When did she finish?

Tess pokes me in the side. "They're calling your name. It's time to go."

"No, I can't do this."

I hear the booming voice again. "Come on, everybody, let's make some noise for Billy Romero. He's our youngest contestant today and may be feeling a bit shy. Let's show him some love."

The crowd starts clapping together. A slow marching sound. The bushy-haired guy is smiling and motioning for me to join him at the podium. This can't be happening.

Tess stands up, then grabs my elbow and helps me to my feet. I can feel the hands of other contestants patting me on the back as they call out words of encouragement. I'm confused; I'm just a kid. Let me be a kid. I'm tired of this constant growing-up routine. Right now it really seems overrated.

Someone gives me a little push toward the podium. Tess says something, but I can't hear her. I walk onto the stage like a marionette. I have no idea who's controlling my strings. My legs feel like they're disconnected from my body; they move awkwardly forward while the rest of my body begs them to run in reverse. As I cross the stage, the crowd starts clapping harder and cheering.

The bushy-haired guy shakes my hand and leaves me alone at the podium. I stare out at the crowd; it's even larger than I thought. There's a bright light shining on my face, and it makes it difficult to see. I feel dizzy again. Just focus on my poem. I look down: It's open and on the podium. When did I do that? Read the first line. Just read it, and then read the next, and when you're done, you can leave and never have to do anything like this ever again.

I look over at Tess. She gives me an encouraging smile and a thumbs-up. Now she's pointing out at the crowd, signaling me to start. I guess I have been looking at her for a while. I can't believe she kissed me like that. What does it mean? Will she want to kiss me again? What about Amy?

It's quiet, although I can hear people beginning to murmur. I know what they're murmuring about. They're murmuring about me. They don't think I can do this. I don't think I can either. Why is this light so bright? Why is "murmur" such an incredibly stupid word?

The crowd's getting louder. I've been standing here too long. Just start reading. Get it over with.

I look down at my poem. Just read it. I move toward the microphone, take a big breath, and plunge in. "'Sometimes late at night, when it's dark / and my dreams have yet to deceive me.'"

I stop. It's like accidentally stepping off the side of a cliff in the dark.

I said "deceive." I was supposed to say "receive." I messed it all up. "Deceive" is totally different from "receive." Do I start over? I can't start over. I messed up my poem. What's wrong with me? I hate this. Why am I here! Why am I doing this? I'm such a loser. I can't believe this.

I look over at Tess. She put down her camera, and she's pointing at the crowd, telling me to keep going. Doesn't she know I messed up the poem? Her lips felt so soft and tender.

This is all her fault. If it weren't for her, I'd be out doing something with Amy or Ziggy today. Her hand moved so lightly across my back. Why couldn't I have gotten Mr. Lippman for English this year?

I gaze out at the crowd. People are starting to murmur again. It's getting even louder than before. How long have I been standing here like this?

Some guy yells, "Deer in the headlights!"

Everyone starts to laugh. Oh, God, I can't believe they're all laughing at me. I've got to get out of here.

I start to run toward Tess. My foot catches on the microphone wire. The floor is suddenly rushing up toward me. I put out my hands to break my fall. There's a loud, hollow *thud* when I hit the wooden floor. It doesn't hurt, more shocking than painful. Everyone's really laughing now.

Tess and the bushy-haired guy rush to my side and help me to my feet. They're both saying something, but I'm not really sure what. Everyone's still laughing.

They're laughing.

They're all laughing at me.

Off the stage I see a large black metal door with a huge red exit sign. That's my goal. That's what I want more than anything in my whole life. My goal is to get from here to that door and the freedom that lies behind it as quickly as possible.

Now, that's something I know I can do.

We pull up in front of Tess's house. I haven't said a word since she found me huddled behind the Dumpster at the theater.

"Billy. I wish you'd talk to me."

I don't want to talk to anyone ever again. When you're quiet, you become invisible. Nobody can hurt you if they can't see you.

"Listen, I know you don't want to go home looking and feeling like this. Come inside, have a cup of hot chocolate, and try to settle down first. Okay?"

I just nod.

Tess has a small yellow house. My mother would call it a "cute Cape." It has green shutters and a large flower garden out front.

She opens the front door; I walk in and just flop down on a couch. There's a pile of laundry next to me, but I don't care. I know I should be looking around right now, saying

172

things like "Oh, what a nice house" and stuff like that, but I'm just not in the mood. All I want to do right now is pull out my sketch pad and draw. Thank God I put it in my backpack this morning.

Tess leans over. "Well, I see you've made yourself at home. Why don't I go make that hot chocolate I promised you?"

I find my roll of pencils and markers, open my pad, and get to work. I start with the bushy-haired guy. Under my direction his hair becomes a nest for rats and spiders; his glasses magnify his mocking eyes. I move on to the audience and turn them into rows and rows of slithering snakes hissing their self-importance.

Tess walks back into the room and looks over my shoulder. "Oh my, you are having some fun, aren't you?"

I just grunt.

She squats down next to the couch; she doesn't say anything for a while. Then she clears her throat. "Billy, I wanted to ask you a favor. I was thinking . . . maybe . . . maybe you shouldn't tell anyone about when we kissed today. They might not understand. It could be our special little secret. Okay?"

They might not understand? I'm not sure *I* understand. But I just look at her. I can hear the microwave squeaking loudly in the other room; I glance in its direction briefly before returning to my drawing.

"Yes, I know," she says. "I don't know what's wrong with it. It works fine; it's just really loud. Do you know how to fix microwaves?"

I give her a simple, "No," but I'm thinking, *Nobody knows how to fix microwaves. They break, you throw them out.*

She puts her hand on my shoulder. "So do we have a deal?"

"I really don't know anything about microwaves."

"Not the microwave. I'm talking about the kiss."

I look up from my drawing. "You mean *kisses*, don't you? Three *kisses*."

She smiles. "Yes, I mean *kisses*. Have we got a deal?"

Maybe those three kisses *should* stay a secret. They don't seem real. There's something about them that feels incredibly strange. Like trying to breathe underwater, or when you wake up in the middle of the night and forget for a moment where you are.

I force myself to smile. "Sure . . . our secret."

The microwave bings in the kitchen. She pats me on the shoulder and heads off to make my hot chocolate.

I start thinking about the regional again. All those people sitting there laughing at me. Why didn't it work out? It's not like I had any grand illusions of winning. It's not like I went in there thinking I was some great poet or anything like that. I just wanted to finish my poem and walk away, that's all.

Tess puts my hot chocolate on the coffee table. "I added some marshmallows. Do you like marshmallows?"

Actually, I don't. I'm not that crazy about hot chocolate, either, so what does it matter? I tell her, "It's fine."

I keep working on my sketch. Tess says something about being embarrassed about her mound of laundry; she sits on the floor and starts to fold it. It seems to be full of very frilly underwear, red thin-type panties, pink bras, sexy lingerie. I can't help but notice. Is this what she wears under her clothes at school every day? Wow, who would have guessed?

She starts folding her gym clothes and socks, and my eyes wander back to my sketch pad. I have to admit this audience full of snakes is looking really good. It just needs a little more detail.

Tess asks, "May I borrow a black and a red marker?"

I hand them to her without looking up. Drawing is helping me relax, but I'm still really angry. What right did those people have to treat me like that? You shouldn't treat anyone like that. I know it's wrong, but I hate them all, especially the bushy-haired guy.

Tess taps me on the shoulder. I say, "What?" but don't look up.

She continues to tap until I look up. I find myself staring into the face of a sock puppet. Tess has taken one of her white tube socks and drawn a face on it with my markers.

In a very high, cartoonish voice she says, "What's the matter, Mr. Billy? Are you saaaaad?"

"I guess."

She rubs the puppet lovingly against my cheek, like a cat does against the leg of its master.

"Oh, Mr. Billy, don't be saaad. Tess told me she wants you to be haaaappy."

I shrug it away. "I'm not in the mood for puppets."

"This puppet wants to tell you that she loooooves you." Tess makes the puppet kiss my face.

"Knock it off."

"Oh, Mr. Billy, don't be like that. Guess what? Tess told me that she really liiiiikes you too. She'll do anything to make you haaaaappy."

"I *said* I don't want to talk to a puppet."

"Oh, Mr. Billy, you're so craaaanky. Okay, be like that. Tess is going to leave you alone in your dark cloud while she takes a quick shower. She'll leave the door open in case you neeeeed anything."

I mumble, "Fine."

She starts to walk away but stops and comes back. The puppet's in my face again. "Mr. Billy. Before I go, kiss me."

The sock puppet starts kissing me all over my face.

I try to push it away.

"Kiss me, you fooool. I know you love socks, I see you with

176

them every day. Admit it, you feeeeel the attraction too."

I continue pushing it away.

"Kiss me, you fooool. Plant one on me. Come on, kiss me. I'm not going to stop until you kiss me."

I start to laugh. This is just too crazy. The puppet's pecking me all over my face and neck.

"Resistance is futile. Kiss meeeeee. Come on, kiss me, kiss me, kiss meeeeee!"

I pucker up and kiss the puppet.

"Ahhhhh, he kissed me! I knew that he loves meeee. I can now go back to the shoe a haaaappy sock."

Tess takes off the puppet and throws it in my lap. "I knew I could get a smile out of you. Don't be sad anymore. Okay? The world didn't end today. Remember, if you need me, I'll be upstairs."

She bounces up the stairs two at a time. I hear her walking around above me. She patters around for a while, then I hear the sound of water and music from the bathroom. I guess she's naked now, the hot water flowing down her body, the soap, the shampoo.

After a while I pick up the sock puppet and slip my hand into it. Tess did a pretty good job with it. She's got some real artistic talent herself. I grab the markers and fill in the eyes better. I make the eyebrows fuller and add some more red to the lips.

I look at it and in a low voice ask, "So, Mr. Puppet, how do you like your new face?"

I use the same voice Tess used. "Oh, thank you, Mr. Billy. I feel ever so much better."

"Mr. Puppet, what do you think Tess meant by she'll leave the door open in case I need anything?"

"I don't know, Mr. Billy. What do yooooou think she meant?"

The phone rings. I jump; then laugh at myself. I think about picking it up, but that would be weird. I wonder if Tess is going to get it, but realize she probably can't hear it. I'll let the machine pick it up. It rings twice, then a third time and a fourth.

It's quiet for a few seconds, then I hear a man's voice booming from the machine's small speaker. "Hey, Tess, it's Dad. Your mom and I just wanted to call and wish you a happy birthday. We were going through some of our old photo albums, and I still can't believe how quickly you grew up. It seems like just yesterday we were taking you home from the hospital. You were the cutest little baby. Anyhow, I love you, your mom loves you, happy birthday. Remember, you'll always be my little girl. Call us back when you get a chance. Bye-bye, sweet pea. We miss you."

What! What! What!

I jump to my feet. I feel like I just looked in the mirror and found a different reflection staring back at me.

Tess's dad? She said her dad was dead. How can this be possible? She lied to me! Why did she lie? Her dad's not dead. All this talk about how she understands how I feel because she's been through it herself is nothing more than a big fat lie!

Is that all this is? Just a lie?

I run up the stairs. There's a door at the end of the hall; it's open a few inches, I can see steam, I hear faint music. I quickly walk toward it. I'm pushing it open and stepping into the bathroom before I even have a chance to think about what I'm doing.

"Tess!"

"I was hoping you'd come up."

I yell, "What's going on?"

She pulls back the curtain. I know she's naked, but I can't let myself look at her body right now. If I look at her body, that's all I'll want to do; it would be like falling into a well. I have to look at her face. I have to look into her eyes. "What's the matter? Why are you so angry?"

"You told me your dad was dead."

Her eyes open wider, she steps backward a little. "He is; he's dead."

"No, he's not, he just called on the phone. He left a message wishing you a happy birthday, and he sounded very much alive."

Tess closes the curtain. "Billy, I'm not dressed. Give me a

second to throw something on and we'll talk. Okay? You're making a huge mistake."

"No, we'll talk right now. Tell me, why did you lie?"

There's a moment of silence, then she turns off the water. "Billy, will you hand me a towel?"

I reach for a towel and notice that I still have the stupid sock puppet on my hand. I angrily rip it off and toss it over the top of the curtain into the shower.

Tess uses her puppet voice again. "Oh, Mr. Billy. I'm all wet. I'm melting. Help meeeeee!"

"Knock it off. Tell me, why did you lie!"

Her voice becomes more serious. More like what she uses at school. "Give me a towel. I'm naked."

I drape a towel over the curtain rod, and she pulls it in.

I demand, "Are you going to tell me why you lied or not?"

"Just a sec."

Tess pulls back the shower curtain. She has the towel wrapped around her body. "Billy, you're getting all upset about nothing. I didn't lie to you. That was my stepfather you heard on the machine."

For a moment I feel incredibly foolish.

I can see the expression on Tess's face changing, shifting from defensive to relieved.

Then I remember what her father said: "It seems like just yesterday we were taking you home from the hospital."

"You're lying again! You're lying! He was talking about when you were a baby!"

Now she looks stunned. She stammers, "Billy, Billy . . . try to . . . try to understand. I only lied because, well, because . . ."

I shout, "I don't want to hear it! This is really sick! Just leave me alone!"

I run out of the bathroom and down the hall. I scramble down the stairs and jump the last five steps but don't realize how low the ceiling is at the bottom. It slams into my forehead. I land on the floor on my back. I struggle to my feet. I'm really dizzy; I can see all these spots dancing before my eyes; my head hurts. I grab my sketch pad and throw it into my backpack. It's like I'm moving in slow motion. I feel something on my forehead, I wipe at it with my hand; it comes back red with blood.

I stumble out the front door. My head's starting to clear; the dizziness is fading away. I'm miles from home, but I don't care. All I want to do is get away from Tess as fast as possible. It looks like all those mornings racing the bus will finally pay off. I tuck my backpack under my arm and explode down the street.

When I'm about a mile from Tess's house, my legs start to feel like rubber bands; I slow to a fast walk. I keep wiping blood off my forehead with the sleeve of my sweatshirt. I can't believe how much it's bleeding.

I'm getting real tired. I slow down to a normal walk. There's still a long way to go before I get home, so I better try to pace myself.

I hear a car roaring up the street and turn around. A moment later it rockets over the ridge in front of me. It's Tess. I think about running, but there's a fence next to me and I'm just too tired to climb over it.

She slams on the brakes; the car fishtails a little before quickly jerking over to the side of the street. I hear a loud, hollow *thud* as she clips one of the fence posts, before coming to a stop in a cloud of dust. I can only imagine what the side of her car must look like now.

"Billy!" Tess jumps from her car. Her hair's still wet and she's wearing her bathrobe. "Billy! Oh, my God. You're really bleeding! Are you okay?"

I shout, "I'm fine! Just leave me alone. I don't want to talk to you!"

She runs to my side. "There was blood all over my living room. Get in the car, Billy. Let me help you. You've got a big cut on your forehead."

I keep walking as fast as my tired legs will move. "Leave me alone. I don't need your help."

She's trying to grab my arm. I keep shrugging her off me. "Come on, Billy. You need some help. You might need stitches."

"Leave me alone! Don't you get it? I don't need you!"

"Billy, please. Don't be like this." She's crying, but her tears don't hold any power over me now. "Try to understand. All I ever wanted to do was help you. From the very first moment I met you, I knew I had to help you. I knew that we were meant to be together. You and I are soul mates. It's written in the stars. We were destined to be together."

Even though I'm tired, I start to run again. Tess reaches out and grabs my arm. She's surprisingly strong. I struggle to free myself from her grip. Her bathrobe comes undone. She's naked underneath.

She pleads, "Please, Billy. You're bleeding. Come with me. I can help you. I love you."

"Let go of me!" It's like my arm is in the mouth of a tiger. The sleeve of my sweatshirt is stretching out.

"Try to understand, I didn't mean to hurt you."

A Jeep Cherokee drives over the ridge, past us, and then slams on its brakes; it pulls over to the side of the road. A second later Mr. Knight and Ziggy jump out.

Mr. Knight booms, "Billy! What's going on here? Are you okay?"

I yell the first thing that comes to my mind. "Help me!"

I'm sitting in a metal folding chair in the Guidance Department. I've spent most of the morning answering questions about Miss Gate. I was crammed into Mr. Knight's office along with six other people I'd never met before and a boxy tape recorder that squeaked louder than a rusty old swing set.

It was really intense; they kept firing questions at me, one right after the other. What they really wanted to know was whether or not we'd ever had sex, except they wouldn't come out and just ask me that. They kept asking all of these other questions, moving in close, then moving away, but never getting to the point. I knew exactly what they really wanted to ask. It was like watching a basketball team that keeps passing around the ball because nobody feels comfortable taking the shot. Finally I just announced that we never had sex.

They all seemed relieved that I had grabbed the ball and taken the shot. I think they were more worried about asking the question than by whatever my answer might be.

Unfortunately, the whole team then decided to rush in for the rebound. "Did she ever kiss you?" "Did you ever see her naked?" "Did she ever say that she loved you?"

Bang, bang, bang, one question right after another.

They seemed mad. Not the yell-and-scream kind of mad, but the kind where the silence crackles louder than the words. I wasn't sure if they were mad at me, or Tess, or just mad that they all had to be there.

My mother's meeting with them now. She's been in there for a while. I actually feel a little sorry for those guys. I don't think they realized what they were inviting into their office. Ever since she found out that Tess lied to her, lied "right to my face," as she puts it, she's been on this major warpath. It's like someone woke up the sleeping giant and now she's stomping on houses all over town.

I'm not sure why they left me waiting out here in this cement-walled purgatory. Maybe they just want me close by in case they have more questions. I don't know. All I know is there's nothing to do here. There's no magazines or books, not even any paper to write on. I'd sell my soul for a sketch pad right now. I'd even settle for a poster to look at. There's absolutely nothing on these walls. It's a guidance office—isn't there some kind of unwritten law that you have to have inspirational posters plastered everywhere?

There's a small window in one of the doors, and I can see out to the main guidance office. I wonder if I should go out there and ask for some paper or something like that?

Chris Dalton's face appears in the window. He looks around like a suspicious shoplifter before quickly opening the door and slipping in. He sits next to me in one of the ancient folding chairs. It creaks and groans whenever he moves.

In a hushed voice I ask, "What are you doing here?"

"Oh, I work in the office. Picking up attendance forms, delivering messages, you know."

I smile. "No, I mean what are you doing in *here?*"

"Oh, I wanted to see how you're doing. The whole school's talking about you."

My head snaps up. "The whole school's talking about *me?*"

"Well, yeah, you and Miss Gate. I heard that she flipped out, took off her clothes, and attacked you, then she carved her initials in your forehead with a knife."

I laugh louder than I have in weeks. I look around, expecting someone to come barging out of one of the offices to see what I'm up to. When nobody comes investigating, I start talking in a normal voice. "Are you serious? Are they really saying things like that?"

"Yeah, really, someone said that Miss Gate was a devil worshipper, and it was some kind of satanic-ritual thing . . . is that true?"

"No, that's insane!"

"Then, what happened to your forehead?"

Without thinking, I reach up and feel the bandage with

the sixteen stitches underneath; it's something I seem to do constantly. I've even started to think of it as my "sweet sixteen."

"I cut it on the ceiling."

"On the ceiling? Yeah, that makes sense. You're, like, what—ten feet tall, right? I can see how ceilings would create a problem. I think I find the whole satanic-ritual thing a little easier to believe."

"Yeah, well, it was the ceiling. I jumped down the stairs and hit the ceiling."

Chris frowns. "Why did you jump down the stairs?"

"Long story."

"I've got time."

Ziggy opens the door and marches in. "Dude! How's it goin'?"

I smile. "Hey, Zig . . . it's starting to look like a party in here." We punch fists as he flops into the last chair; it makes a popping sound but doesn't collapse.

He leans forward. "Hey, Chris, what's new and different?"

I'm sitting between them, so Chris just motions at me with his thumb. "Well, he's different. I'm trying to figure out what happened. He claims there were no satanic rituals involved, but I'm not really convinced."

"Did he give you that story about cutting his head on the ceiling?"

The two of them laugh.

I shrug. "Well, that's what happened. What do you want me to do, lie?"

Chris leans forward and asks Ziggy, "Do you know what happened to him?"

I put up my hands. "Hello? I'm right here. Why don't you ask me?"

"Well, I've been trying to. What happened?"

"It's . . . it's kinda complicated."

Chris rolls his eyes and leans forward again. "Zig, I heard you and your dad took him to the hospital. What happened?"

Ziggy's eyes fly open wide. "Dude, it was so crazy. My dad and I were coming back from McDonald's. I had a Big Mac in one hand and a Coke in the other. We're just talking and stuff. We drive over this hill, and there's Billy on the side of the street. He's got blood all over his face, and Miss Gate is trying to pull him into her car. She's wearing nothing but a bathrobe, and it's wide open. You could see *everything.*"

Chris says, "Oh God, *everything?*"

"Yeah . . . *everything.*"

"Oh, I would have loved to see that!"

I look at Chris. "What, me bleeding?"

"No, you moron, not you bleeding, Miss Gate's naked body. She's hot. Zig, did she have a knife, too?"

"No, she didn't have a knife. But she looked like she

was out of her English-teaching mind. She was yelling and shouting all sorts of crazy things."

"Really? Like what?"

"Oh, I couldn't make it all out. My dad wanted me to get Billy into the Jeep. We've got a first-aid kit, so I was kinda focused on getting him bandaged up. But from what I heard, it sounded like she'd completely lost it. She kept yelling, 'But we're soul mates.' It was scary.

"Billy wanted us to just take him home. I couldn't believe it. He's, like, just sitting there, covered in blood, looking like an extra from a low-budget horror film, and he's saying, 'Oh, I'm fine. It's just a little cut.' My dad drove him straight to the hospital. They gave him sixteen stitches."

Chris looks at my forehead. "You got sixteen stitches?"

"Yeah."

"Did it hurt?"

"A little."

"What did your mom say?"

Ziggy can't seem to control himself. He takes over, and they talk around me as if I'm not even there. "Oh, dude, you should have seen it! When his mom got there, she just *freaked out*. I mean totally, completely freaked out. She was yelling and screaming at my dad about Miss Gate. Later when the cops came, she kept yelling, "I want that woman arrested!" It was really, really crazy. The whole thing was just crazy. That's the only word for it: crazy."

Chris shakes his head. "Did they arrest Miss Gate?"

"No, not yet. I know the cops have been talking to her. My dad said these things take time. They've got to gather evidence and stuff like that."

"Evidence? What kind of evidence? What did she do?"

"I'm not sure." Ziggy looks at me. "What kind of evidence are they looking for?"

I stare at the two of them. I can't believe how my story is being passed around the school like the church's offering plate. If everybody adds something, it's definitely going to grow beyond these walls. I don't want this to turn into one of those stories you see running on cable news all day long. I don't want my mother to go through that.

I shrug. "I don't even understand what's going on myself, and that's the truth."

I stand up. I've got to get out of here.

"Listen, I've gotta go to the bathroom. If anyone comes looking for me, tell them I'll be right back."

Ziggy hands me a piece of paper. "Here, take my hall pass."

I bolt out of the room and run down the empty hall. I turn the corner and practically slam right into Miss Gate. The two of us jump backward with these silly startled expressions on our faces. I feel something inside of me swell from my chest to my head. She's the last person I expected to see right now. I don't know how to act or what to say or even whether or not I should smile. I'm confused, aggravated, and nervous all at the same time.

Nick, the security guard, is standing by her side. They're both holding large cardboard boxes.

A few years ago Nick was one of the best high school football players in the state. There were scouts from all the major universities watching him. Then something happened to his knee. Now if he weren't so big, I doubt anybody would even notice when he walked into a room.

Tess seems a whole lot calmer than the last time I saw her. I flash back and picture the wild look in her eyes and all the crazy things she was yelling that afternoon. It doesn't help me relax.

"Tess, hey, um . . . how's it going?"

She stares over the edge of her large cardboard box. She seems as uncomfortable as I feel. "Hi, Billy . . . I'm just here to collect my stuff. You know Nick, he's . . . helping me."

"Hey, Nick."

He just grunts.

It looks like she's about to put the box down, but she changes her mind. "I've only got a second. My lawyer doesn't want me to talk to you, but I just wanted you to know that I never meant you any harm."

It feels strange talking about lawyers with Nick towering over us, and even stranger trying to talk with this large brown box between us. I think of it as the first block in a wall that's only going to grow larger with time.

Nick clears his throat. "Uh, Miss Gate. I think we should get moving. We're supposed to clear your desk, then leave the building."

She turns and stares at him. That's all she does, just stares. After a while this big man somehow seems to start to shrink, to implode. Finally his gaze falls to the floor.

"Nick, all I want is one minute. That's not too much to ask for. Nobody said anything about gagging me. Besides, you're standing right here—what's going to happen?"

He grunts, "Okay . . . make it quick."

"Thank you for understanding. You're an angel."

Then she smiles the most beautiful smile I've ever seen before. It's like she cast a spell, and Nick seems to grow back to his old height right before my eyes. Then he does something I've never seen him do before: He smiles.

She raises her eyebrows and they somehow move Nick about six feet away. He squats against a locker with the box by his side.

I want to tell her what's bothering me, so I just blurt out, "Tess, I'm worried this whole thing's about to get turned into one of those sick stories that gets plastered all over the news. I don't want photographers following me around or camped out in my front yard. I don't want my mom and the twins to have to go through that. I think it would be too much for everyone."

Pop, pop, pop, snap, snap.

Nick found some bubble wrap in Tess's box, and he's popping the plastic bubbles. Tess glares over at him, but he's too busy to notice her glare.

She lets out a long sigh. "Don't worry. I wouldn't let anybody hurt you. I hope you know that. This is all smoke and no fire."

Snap, pop, pop, pop . . . snap.

"I think you should know that I've worked out a deal. I'm going to quietly resign and move out of town. This is all getting way out of hand. It's time for me to step forward and make it stop."

Pop, pop . . . snap, pop.

"My lawyer thinks I'm crazy . . . but I think it's for the best. If you can keep your mother from pressing this forward, I think it will all go away."

Snap, snap, pop, pop, pop.

"Do you think you can get her to do that?"

Pop. Pop. Snap.

I have so many different questions I'd like to ask, but I know I never will, so instead I just say, "I think I can do that."

Snap, pop, snap, pop.

"Then, we shouldn't have any more problems."

"I guess."

Snap, snap, pop, pop.

We stand awkwardly together in the empty hall while

Nick continues to pop the bubble wrap. The tension starts to thicken. Finally she gives me a very weak smile. "It looks like this is good-bye."

"I guess."

Pop, pop, snap.

"Billy . . . I . . . well, just good-bye."

Snap, pop, pop.

"Bye, Tess."

She turns to Nick. "Okay, are you *through?* I think we can get going now."

He picks up the box, and the two of them start to walk away, but Tess stops and turns around. "Do me a favor. Whenever you come across Orion in the night sky, remember the story I told you and think of me."

"Okay . . . I'll try."

"Take care of yourself, Billy Romero."

"Take care, Tess."

I watch her walk down the long hall. Her heels tapping on the tile floor, her skirt swaying with each step, her hair bouncing on her shoulders. Nick opens the door at the end of the hall. Sunlight rushes in and surrounds them, and they disappear into its bright embrace. The door slams shut behind them.

She never looked back.

Dear Dad,

Well, it's been a while since my last letter. I wanted to write you on the anniversary of your death, but that was an incredibly painful day, too painful to pick up a pen. It was harder than I would have thought. It might have been harder for Mom. I'm not sure. We sat together on the couch watching a movie, but mainly we just stared off into that place where memories are kept, poisoned by our hunger to have you back.

There's still a lot of sadness in the house. I can feel it when I move from room to room; it's a deep, hollow darkness. It comes and it goes, but if you're not careful, you can fall right into it. I never go in your old den. It's too difficult. It's just as you left it; the only thing missing is you. Little things remind me of you too—the hook on the bathroom door, the shelves in the hall, the tile floor in the kitchen, all the things you've worked on, built, or repaired.

I thought the pain would have lessened by now, but it hasn't. It still cuts and burns and presses down upon me. The only difference is I now recognize this uninvited stranger who refuses to go. I've learned to live with his darkness and sorrow. Sometimes when he walks into a room, I even find the strength to stand up and leave.

Bragg says I'm doing much better. He cut our visits down to every other week. I hope he doesn't cut them down further, at least not for a while. I kinda like Dr. Bragg. He's taught me how to think things through and to understand what I can and can't control.

A few months ago my friend Chris Dalton lost his mother. She had lung cancer. He fell apart for a while. The sadness wrapped itself around him, but I was there for him every day.

He blamed himself for not making her stop smoking. I know all about blaming yourself, but there's so much more that I don't understand. Everything's like a jigsaw puzzle, where you have to hunt for the pieces before you can put it together. Maybe Chris and I can help each other hunt for the missing pieces. Maybe some pieces are lost forever. I just don't know.

Chris seems to be doing better. Bragg said he had a long time to try to come to grips with the situation, but added that I've been a huge help.

One day his father pulled me aside and thanked me for helping Chris. I found myself wondering if I would have been there for him if I hadn't lost you. I doubt I would have. What does that say about me? Nothing really, I guess.

The trouble with my old English teacher, Tess Gate, faded away, unlike the scar on my forehead. I decided I wasn't going to talk about her, and after a while everyone else stopped too.

I haven't heard anything from her. Except for something strange that happened on my birthday. I received a small package in the mail with no return address. When I opened it, all I found was a sock puppet, no note or card, just a sock puppet. I know she's the one who sent it. I wanted to throw it away but didn't. It's in a box buried deep in the back of my closet.

Amy and I have been together for six months now. I just bought her a necklace with a little gold heart on it. Well, Mom actually paid for it, but I picked it out. I'm going to give it to her tonight.

Last week I was throwing away a bunch of these old

VHS tapes. I came across one that wasn't marked. When I put it in the player, I thought it was blank at first. Just when I was about to take it out, a picture came on. It was you and me. I must have been about four or five. You were teaching me how to play baseball. I guess Mom was taping it. I'm standing there with this bat on my shoulder, and you keep slowly lobbing balls over the plate.

You say, "Come on, Billy, swing. You can do it."

I just stand there. Finally I take this huge swing and hit one. It surprises everyone by sailing right by you. I hear Mom laughing behind the camera. You have this stunned expression on your face.

Mom yells, "That's your boy!"

After a moment you look at me and yell, "Now, run, Billy. Run to first base!"

I start to run and giggle at the same time. The camera starts shaking as it follows me. A second later it cuts off.

That's all there was on the tape, just that four-minute clip. I think I must have watched it about twenty times. I just kept rewinding and playing it over and over.

Dad, it didn't make me sad. I was just happy that we both shared that moment. There were thousands of moments just like that one. I'm grateful for each and every one of them. I'm so lucky to have had such a great dad. I promise I'll never forget you.

I miss you.

I love you.

I'll always try to make you proud.

Summertime

"What's taking so long?" I yell.

Amy shouts, "Give me a sec, I want to make sure it's perfect."

I turn to Ziggy. "Are you scared?"

"Nah . . . well, maybe just a little."

Chris laughs. "I'm not scared. I'm beyond scared. What's beyond scared?"

I shrug. "Petrified?"

Ziggy starts laughing. "Isn't that like when wood turns into stone?"

"Yeah, I guess."

Amy yells, "Okay! I'm all set!"

Chris looks at me. "We really going to do this?"

"We sure are. . . . Zig, you ready?"

"Ready as I'll ever be."

"Okay, on three." I yell loud enough for Amy to hear, "Okay! Here we come. One . . . two . . . three!"

We run across a short patch of grass. The edge of the

cliff quickly approaches. Beyond the edge lies the sky. I can see treetops and the other side of the lake. It's even higher than I remember. I quickly glance at Ziggy and Chris as we all reach the edge at the same time, and without hesitation we launch ourselves over the side.

I start to laugh. The wind is rushing past us. I move my arms to keep myself balanced. We seem to be moving both in slow motion and faster than I've ever moved before.

Ziggy shouts out, "Oh, yeaaaah!" His hair is standing straight up as we rush toward the water.

I glance over to the shore and see Amy with her camera and a huge smile.

Chris is laughing. There's a nervous smile plastered on his face.

I see our reflections in the water. We're rushing toward each other. I wonder if the water will hurt. I hold my legs together, point my toes, and take one final breath.

I plunge deep into the water, and it doesn't hurt at all. It feels so good. It's cold, dark, and quiet. I can see the sun sparkling on the surface far above me. It looks like thousands and thousands of twinkling stars. It's stunning, unlike anything I've ever seen before. Then I hear Tess's voice: *"Do me a favor. Whenever you come across Orion in the night sky, remember the story I told you and think of me."*

I push her voice out of my head; I push away her kisses, her lies; I push away all the time we spent together. I swim hard for the surface of stars, *my* stars; I'm rising toward them like a rocket. I break through and gasp in a fresh breath of air. I feel the warmth of the sun on my face. I hear the laughter of friends. I feel alive and well.

Ziggy yells, "Dude, that was awesome!"

Chris smiles. "I must have been petrified, because I fell like a stone."

I look over at Amy. "Did you get it?"

She's looking into the camera with Julie and their friend Karen. She gives me a thumbs-up.

"Billy . . . you guys look great!"

I turn over and float on my back and look up into the deep blue sky. The sun feels so comforting. I let everything drift out of my mind—everything that's happened with my father, with Tess, and with all this pain that's held me so tightly. I listen to myself breathe, and I relax. I focus just on the sky and this floating sensation; I smile and think: *Yes, this is what it would be like to be a balloon.*